BREAKING WITH

HIS PAST

by James Lee Hard

BREAKING WITH HIS PAST

For questions and comments about this book, please contact the author at jamesleehard@jamesleehard.com or at www.jamesleehard.com.

For news about new books, sign my newsletter at http://eepurl.com/bgofyb

WARNING

This book contains explicit sexual scenes as well as some graphic language. It is intended for a mature, adult audience.

ISBN-13: 978-1537504391
ISBN-10: 1537504398

Other books by James Lee Hard

Stripped Expectations *

The Groom, the Bride and the Best Man (short story)

Becoming Jake *

Falling for Matt *

The Rift series

Jason's Fall (The Rift Book 1)
The Nephilim's Calling (The Rift Book 2)
Master's Revenge (The Rift Book 3)

*Available in paperback

Special note from the author

Thank you for reading my stories and supporting me. I really appreciate it and can only thank you for that. You are the best readers in the world!

If you have the time, please consider leaving a review on Amazon, as this helps indie authors a lot. Also, thank you so much to my beta readers whose input is, as always, invaluable.

To you, my love.

Prologue

The rusty hinges screeched and echoed on the street as the prison guard opened the heavy gate. Logan was one step away from becoming a free man. Outside this cold building, he would start over and forget about the miserable years spent in this place. Logan glanced at the prison guard, who observed him with nothing more than a glint of indifference in his eyes. He'd no doubt seen too many convicts being set free only to return to their former lives and inevitably back into jail to feel any real empathy for Logan's fate.

Logan took a deep breath to ease his anxiety and walked out. In front of him was a vast, empty expanse of parking lot, around it a green belt of trees. The air almost stood still but for the faint hum of the nearby highway. The sun above shone bright and hot. Logan had already forgotten how it could burn outside the confines of his prison cell. In the jail's courtyard the sun somehow always seemed dimmer.

The squealing sound of the closing gate behind him pulled Logan back to reality, and he headed out to the bus stop, to check the schedule. He found he'd have to wait.

He sat on a bench, took a piece of paper out of his pocket and unfolded it. His care officer had scribbled down the name of a shelter that helped people like him. He scoffed. People like him. He'd meant it to mean those who wanted to start their lives afresh, to return to society as an upright citizen, but Logan could only think of the word "ex-convict". He saved the details in his pocket again and closed his eyes, tilting his head up to feel the sun warming his skin, its fiery glow penetrating his eyelids. Being outside still felt like a dream, and Logan feared that if he opened his eyes it would all vanish before him. His mind now began working on a plan. The bus would take him to the city center, after which he'd find the shelter, and then... Who knew? He just hoped he could start again, preferably as far away as possible from his former life.

Logan was beginning to doze off when the arrival of the bus startled him. The driver opened the door and Logan blinked at the man now staring down at him and got up. He paid his fare and searched for an empty seat, somehow excited and nervous at the same time about this new chapter of his life, one that was starting at this very moment.

The short trip to the city center, though, didn't let him dwell too much on how things would be from here on in. As he exited the bus, a sea of people engulfed him and Logan felt lightheaded. There were so many of them, a stark contrast to his days in prison, the few same old faces around him for five years. He drew in a deep breath and tried to ground himself, to ignore the buzz of the crowd. Should he go left or right? But then, Logan noticed how no one cared about him, how he was just another faceless soul amongst them.

It was time; time to start over.

Chapter One

Logan's arms began to ache. He flexed them again before once more running the block plane over the board. Wood trimmings as thin as paper flew off the tool. They were exactly the thickness he was aiming for, and so he continued his work. Precision was the hardest part of the job, but it was also where he excelled. And in the last five years, Logan had found himself with plenty of time to practice. There hadn't been much else to do in prison.

"It's time to go home. Wanna grab a drink first?"

Logan drew his gaze away from the workbench and to the workshop's door. His boss, Kurt Shaffer, nodded at him while drying his hands vigorously on a rag. The light behind him was dwindling and Logan realized the day was coming to an end.

"Thanks, but I'm staying a while longer. I wanna finish this."

The barrel-chested man shrugged and turned around. "Okay. Just don't forget to lock up before leaving."

Logan nodded.

The sound of a door closing echoed through the empty room. He sighed and gazed at the piece of wood firmly gripped in the tail vise, then resumed trimming it and ignored the fading day outside. His life had been a blur since getting out of jail on parole six months earlier, each day the same as the one before. He worked hard and tried not to think of the years he'd wasted behind bars. He couldn't change what had happened and so it didn't make any sense to dwell on it. The only thing he could do now was to focus on his future and try to live a straight life.

Logan blew the shavings off the wood. He caressed the board with his large hands and his calloused fingers made the wood sing with a soothing tone. That sound told him his work was done. Behind him, a neat pile of boards awaited being assembled into a bespoke cupboard. He released the wood from the tail vise and stowed it away, trying to decide if he was going to work the extra hours and assemble the cupboard that evening or not. He'd been having suffocating nightmares about his time in prison, waking up drenched in sweat. So he worked himself to exhaustion in the hope of getting a dreamless night for once.

Those first few weeks in jail still haunted him. The alpha males would mark their territory by humiliating both the newcomers and the weaklings amongst the prisoners. Logan had defended himself as best he could and made sure no one in there took him for some defenseless virgin, ripe for the picking. One night he'd woken up with an elephantine man on his back, breathing on his neck, droplets of the guy's sweat falling onto Logan's cheek. The man whispered he was going to rip his ass open, his putrid breath assaulting Logan's nostrils and making him feel sick. The jolt of fear and adrenaline had made him muster a strength he didn't even know he had. The guy was already trying to pull his pants down when Logan elbowed him hard on the nose. While the guy leaned back in pain, Logan took the chance to turn himself around and push him so hard he'd fallen back, hit his head and had to be taken to the infirmary. After that, Logan had gotten a couple of threats for what he'd done, but no one went near him.

He shook his head, trying to get rid of the nightmarish images that insisted on resurfacing. He grabbed a few of the boards and lifted them with ease. They probably weighed some hundred pounds altogether, but he was strong enough. The free gym had been one of the few perks of being incarcerated. After carefully placing them on the assembly table, he took a step back. What was he doing? Working himself this hard, he now decided, wasn't really helping with the nightmares. So why was he here instead of going home? Logan still didn't quite know how to answer that question.

"Enough for today," he mumbled to himself.

Taking his work apron off, he went to wash his hands in a small sink. After drying them, he grabbed his jacket and turned off the lights. Shaffer & Hamilton Woodworks specialized in all kinds of upscale wood pieces beyond furniture, and Logan was becoming a key element in the company's success. His attention to detail and love for the craft was finally paying off. He locked the doors and left the building.

The tepid, late-afternoon breeze gently whispered in the leaves of the trees, stirring the birds that flocked around, chirping and fighting for a spot to spend the night. The golden light that slipped through the branches bathed the street in its rich, warm colors. Around him, people were busy returning home. A small group of children played catch nearby, something Logan had thought was a rarity these days. But such was Greenville, a small and safe town where everybody knew each other. It had a familiarity to it that Logan had never felt before, and certainly not in his hometown. The streets back home were no place for a child to be, unless they were up to something or their parents had been arrested by the police. Logan remembered being really young, maybe ten or eleven, and seeing a thirteen-year old stab another kid over some silly argument. Street rules dictated that in order to maintain an iron grip you had to beat anyone who dared defy you. But even then, Logan knew that stabbing was too extreme, especially for a kid.

He headed out to his 1971 Ford F-100, feeling the warm air on his skin and nodding at occasional passersby. The pickup truck was an old clunker he'd bought a couple of months earlier. It wasn't in the greatest of conditions. Some would have said it was a death trap, but it was the only car he could afford.

"Oh, hi, Mr. Logan," he heard a woman's voice say as he was about to open the door to his Ford. Logan turned around.

"Hi, Ms. Sarah. How are you tonight?" and he smiled, trying to be polite. He didn't know the woman that well, beyond that she was spending more and more time in the store. She and a couple of her friends had flocked to Shaffer & Hamilton Woodworks a little after Logan had begun working there.

"I've been meaning to pass by the store to talk to you about some ideas for my new porch."

Sarah took a step forward and was now a foot away from Logan. He could see crow's feet in her otherwise smooth skin and tried to guess her age. She seemed past thirty-five but he couldn't be sure. The only thing on his mind right now was her spicy perfume that wafted through the air and overwhelmed his nostrils. She was too close. It was uncomfortable.

"Sure thing, Ma'am. I'll tell Mr. Shaffer you need to talk to him." Logan nodded and opened the truck's door, intending to leave, but Sarah approached and touched his arm.

"I was hoping to discuss my needs with you."

The women here were becoming cheekier by the day. He smiled politely. "I only build things, Ma'am. You should talk to Mr. Shaffer. 'Night."

Before Sarah could say anything else, Logan climbed into his truck and shut the door. As he put the keys in the ignition, he looked through the window and again nodded at Sarah. She was watching him with a mix of surprise and anger. Maybe it was the way he'd spoken to her but he really didn't care. Entertaining her fantasies wasn't in his list of priorities.

As he drove away, Logan thought of how it was getting harder to ignore the advances of women. He wasn't ashamed of being gay but he was starting a new life in a small town and feared people wouldn't be so welcoming if they knew. He cranked the window open and let the wind clear his mind and caress his short hair. He missed the touch of a man but Greenville wasn't exactly the kind of place to search for a quick lay, or for love, for that matter. Most of the people here were married churchgoers. The others were widowers or hermits. He probably should have moved to a younger town, but Greenville was just what he needed in his life right now: a small, secluded place away from everything where no one knew him or his past. Besides, it had been the only place he'd been able to find a job.

Logan turned into the narrow road that led to his house just outside town, a cottage-style place in dire need of a fresh coat of paint. But he'd fallen in love with it as soon as he saw the vistas from the front porch. He immediately imagined himself sitting there, drinking beer and enjoying a warm summer night. Of course, he'd visited it during a crisp winter's day and hadn't really thought about how it would be in the miserable rainy months. The unpaved road still looked like a Swiss cheese from last spring's rainfall.

The air was thick with the scents of this part of the county's forest and he loved it. It had been one of the reasons he'd chosen to rent the house. As he approached the final stretch of his route, he saw Mrs. Cook on her driveway, unloading groceries from her car. She was his only neighbor for miles around, the other reason that had led him to choose this place. He turned into her drive. Mrs. Cook was a sweet lady who lived there all by herself. More often than not, Logan ended up helping her with her chores. How could he not? Besides, she had been nothing but welcoming since he'd arrived. He fondly remembered the hot meal she'd brought him on his first night here, as a welcome neighborly gift, so to speak. It ended up being a godsend for he'd just realized his pantry was empty.

"Hi, Mrs. Cook. Let me give you a hand," he said, pulling up next to her.

Mrs. Cook smiled at him. "Thank you, dear. I don't wanna be any trouble." Her voice was small and frail, but she was a tough old lady who spent her days around her garden. She reminded him of his grandmother with her short, curly white hair, although he didn't remember her very well. She'd died when he was young, maybe six or seven years old. He couldn't say for sure.

"It's no trouble at all." Logan turned off his truck's engine, opened the door and hopped out. "You should buy your groceries online and have someone deliver them to you," he said as he went around the truck.

Mrs. Cook laughed. "Buy my groceries online? And have them deliver me wilted produce? I prefer to choose my own apples, thank you very much. Besides, I could never make one of those damn computer things work properly, anyway. Imagine; I'd end up with my groceries being sent to another town."

Logan grabbed the grocery bags and kissed Mrs. Cook on the cheek. "I can teach you. You'd be surfing the web in no time."

"Thank you, dear, but I think I prefer to tend to my gladiolus than go on the internet." Mrs. Cook unlocked her door and, turning around, said, "It's funny. I just came from my granddaughter's house and she told me the same thing. Maybe I should introduce you. You'd make a fine couple."

Logan smiled, feeling torn between asking Mrs. Cook what she had in mind for a possible grandson and being polite. "I think your granddaughter would be better off with someone else, someone less of a backwoodsman."

"Nonsense. You're nothing like that."

"That's how I feel, these days." Logan placed Mrs. Cook's bags on the kitchen counter. When he turned around, he found her gazing at him, a knowing look on her face.

"Well, thank you for your help, dear," she said, placing her wrinkly hand on his arm. "Need anything for your supper?"

"No, ma'am. Have a good night." And with a nod, he left. Logan had a distinct feeling Mrs. Cook had read him beyond his lame excuse but there was nothing he could do about it. Or wanted to. His desire to stay below Greenville's folk's radar didn't mean he would all of a sudden become straight.

He arrived at his own driveway a couple of miles later. Turning off the engine, he saw a black shadow zooming toward him, followed by a series of barks.

"Hey, Buddy," he said, laughing, as he got out of the truck. Logan crouched, arms open. Buddy, a black mutt, responded with excited barks and jumped into his arms, happier than ever and licking Logan's face. "Did you miss me? I know, it's late. Come on. I'll fix you something to eat." He stood and gestured for Buddy to follow him.

Logan had adopted the dog shortly after arriving in town. One day, after work, he'd been about to leave when he saw Buddy lying by his truck, his drooping ears making him look miserable and irresistible all at the same time. The dog had lifted his head and gently whined at him, like he was asking for help. Logan felt sorry for the poor mutt and petted him. Buddy returned the favor by licking his hand and Logan fell in love right there. It had been a love story ever since.

Logan went inside and into the kitchen, Buddy jumping around him. He grabbed a biscuit bag from the pantry and gave one to Buddy who snatched it from his hand and ate it happily. Once devoured, the dog looked up, an inquiring look in his eyes, as if asking for more.

"Easy there. That was only a treat. Dinner is coming right up."

Buddy woofed and sat, as if waiting for his meal. Logan chuckled and grabbed a big, thirty-pound bag of dry food and emptied a portion into a metal bowl.

"Go easy on it or you'll get fat. You have to be mindful of your health, you hear me?"

The pooch ignored him, of course, too busy munching his dinner. Logan petted him on his rump and left him to eat his food. Buddy was new in his life but gave him easy company, greeting him with nothing but love and enthusiasm every time Logan arrived home. He couldn't imagine himself without him.

"If only I'd bumped into a guy like you, Buddy," he said to himself. He went upstairs and changed into his running outfit, although he knew he shouldn't exercise in the evening, not if he wanted to get a good night sleep. He felt anxious, though, and needed to burn off some of that excess energy. The nightmares were taking their toll. Not only was he having trouble sleeping, now he was also beginning to get anxious about it before going to bed. And he couldn't let them take over his life. This was a new chapter. There was no reason to let his past steer his present. He would get over it.

Chapter Two

The day was coming to an end and a warm breeze was picking up. Kyle stepped out of the car with a sigh. The house stood in front of him, big and dark, and he realized he hadn't been here in almost a year, the place which was supposed to be their retreat from the big city. At least, that was what Jessica had wanted. For him, the place had always been a nuisance. He'd even thought of selling it, given it was in the middle of nowhere and the last place he wanted to be. But now? Now he was thankful he still owned it.

Kyle opened the car trunk and grabbed his trolley and backpack. His entire life fitted inside these two bags, which was funny when he thought of all the stuff he'd had in his former home. The only thing missing was his son but the separation had been ugly enough. It would be unfair for him to drag Ryan away from his mother. It broke his heart to say it, but the little guy would be better off with her for the time being. Kyle needed to sort his head out before thinking of having his son with him again.

He closed the trunk and went inside with his things. Everything was covered in dust and Kyle sneezed loudly as soon as he closed the door behind him. Leaving the trolley and backpack in the entrance hall, he went into the living room and opened the windows. The fresh air immediately made him feel better, as if all those months of stale, dusty air were being sucked away. The place was mostly empty as it had never really been used fulltime. He would need new furniture to make it his home, though, but that could wait. Right now he had to get rid of this sooty air. After opening every window on the ground floor, Kyle went upstairs and did the same up there. When he arrived in the bedroom, he was pleased to see he'd had the good sense to cover the bed with large sheets the last time he was here. Had it been the previous summer? He couldn't remember. If he removed them carefully, he could avoid covering the bed in a thick layer of dust and waking up the next day with a runny nose and puffy eyes. The whole place was in dire need of a deep scrub but he needed to prioritize. And that meant at least cleaning the bedroom before nightfall.

Kyle spent a good couple of hours scrubbing it. There had still been some house supplies in the kitchen, so he'd rolled up his sleeves and got to work. He'd always hated cleaning but the menial task had the advantage of taking his mind off things. For the past couple of days he hadn't been able to stop thinking about how he'd blown everything. He shouldn't have had that talk with Jessica, his wife. Maybe he should've kept ignoring his feelings and the pain that was tearing a hole inside him. He had dealt with questions and doubts about himself for so long. Why had he gone and messed things up when his life was supposedly so good? Was he selfish? Was that it? He had a job, a family, a nice house… His life had been picture-perfect and still he'd felt that worm of doubt gnawing in his mind, persuading him to speak with Jessica and tell her the truth about his sexuality. And he finally had, even though it was painfully difficult just to think about it now. He couldn't even say he was gay in his own mind. How was he supposed to say it out loud to Jessica? He played their conversation over and over in his mind, and in his scenario Jessica would understand and they'd end up on friendly terms—after the initial shock, of course. In reality, though, things hadn't quite go as he'd expected.

His stomach growled at him. The room was done and he was starving. After bringing his belongings up, Kyle drove off to the city. Tonight he would eat out. Tomorrow, he'd fill up his pantry and think of cleaning the rest of the house.

***

Kyle drove to a burger place downtown where he'd eaten in the last time he'd been in the city. He worried it would be full and he'd have to search for somewhere else, but it was fairly empty when he walked in. In another lifetime, he wouldn't even have considered going in. Empty restaurants were empty for a reason. But this night was different. He was exhausted and hungry, and wanted to go to sleep and forget the three-hour drive he'd had and the new life he was about to embark upon. Plus, he had eaten here before and the food wasn't that bad.

He sat at a table and scanned the place. Wooden beams from floor to ceiling gave the restaurant a touch of hunting cabin. All the tables had little lamps that lent a cozy, intimate feeling to the place and faded the people around him. The handful of customers all seemed to be out-of-towners as well. Kyle didn't remember the restaurant like this but, then again, it had been a while since he'd last been here.

A girl approached the table a couple of minutes later. She was chewing gum with her mouth open, sporting a big smile and looking like she wasn't a day over eighteen. Her T-shirt showed her belly button and seemed a number too small. Her skimpy skirt didn't do her any favors, either.

"Welcome to Jeff's. I'm Stacy and I'll be your waitress tonight. Can I get you started with some water or a drink?"

Her voice and personality were too bubbly and sugary. She reminded him of his days in high school when he'd felt pressured to go out with girls like her. The "Woo-girls", as they'd called them, because of their constant excited screams. Everything had been about scoring and proving you were a real man, even if the truth was they were all scared kids and none of them knew what they were doing. But an act had to be put on, one that hid how afraid they were.

The girl was now staring at him with a weird expression. Kyle pulled up his big, charming smile and tried to ignore her. "Can you bring me a beer, please? And a house burger with fries." Stacy took note of his order but was still looking at him, as though she wanted to say something. "Is everything okay?" he ended up asking. He wasn't really sure he wanted to know but old habits die hard, as they say, and Kyle had engaged his inner charming-straight-guy without realizing it. The girl was probably staring over something silly. He most likely reminded her of a younger Joe Manganiello. It happened a lot, although Kyle didn't think he looked anything like him.

She blushed and stammered, seeming embarrassed, as though she hadn't noticed she'd been staring. "I'm... I'm so sorry. I didn't mean to be rude. I was just trying to guess your age because you seem really young but then you have that little white patch above your forehead, which threw me off. I'm real sorry."

The white hair was a recent thing. Sometime after talking to Jessica and the fights that had ensued, he had woken up to find a patch of white hair above his forehead. He'd ended up reasoning that it was from the stress, as no one else in his family had anything like it.

"That's okay. I get that a lot."

Stacy chuckled. "Did you dye it?"

"No, it's natural."

"It suits you," she said, blushing again. "If you need anything else, I'll be around." She left with something akin to an embarrassed giddiness. As she was putting her order up, another waitress approached her. Kyle saw them from across the room, exchanging words and looking over at him. He let out a long sigh. He really had to stop being all flirty with girls. It had been his defense mechanism since he could remember, but it had to stop. That wasn't the real him.

Kyle grabbed his phone. He had a couple of missed calls from Jessica. For a moment there, he couldn't understand why he hadn't heard them come in but then realized the phone had been on silent since god knew when. Shit. He dialed his voicemail and listened as Jessica raged on about how she'd thrown his clothes out and that her apartment wasn't his personal storage room. Kyle pinched the bridge of his nose and hung up. A wave of outrage washed over him but he tried to stay calm. Jessica was in her right to be angry. It was his fault for having brought all this drama on them. He'd known something like this could happen from the moment he'd said he was leaving. But he had to. They couldn't continue living under the same roof, not after what they'd both said. They'd agreed it was the best thing for them, and for Ryan.

"Here's your beer."

Stacy's voice brought Kyle back from his musings.

"Thanks."

"Is everything all right? You look a bit pale."

Kyle mustered all his remaining energy. "I'm just tired. It's been a very long day and I think I need a good night's sleep more than I realized."

Stacy seemed disappointed. "I'll see if I can rush your order."

"Thanks."

He watched as Stacy made her way to the kitchen and wondered why she had seemed disappointed. It didn't matter anyway. He just wanted to eat something and go to sleep for a week. The day really had been long and he felt like he'd been up for ages. Kyle unlocked his phone again and opened his Facebook app. His feed was filled with the usual posts about cats and political rantings. There were a few private messages and a couple of people had posted on his wall, asking if he was okay and wondering what was going on. There were also those, mostly Jessica's friends, who accused him of being a bad husband. Kyle scoffed and deleted the posts. Those idiots weren't really close friends. More like acquaintances he'd met through Jessica. Maybe he should unfriend them. He never really understood how people could talk about their lives on social media like that. Kyle stared at the private messages' icon for a moment, trying to decide if he should read them. Opening Messenger, he stared at the messages without opening them. He could see his friends were worried about him by the way their texts began. His friends. Kyle's relationship with them was bittersweet. He liked most of them but didn't know if they were really his friends. How could they be if he'd never opened up to any of them? He'd done some pretty stupid things in his life.

He sighed and put the phone away. He would read and answer their messages later. Right now, he just wanted to eat something and pretend the day had never happened.

Chapter Three

The wind picked up as soon as Logan went out through the green metal gate. Dead leaves swirled up from the ground. The cotton-cloudy sky loomed dark above, almost slate-blue as it threatened to open its celestial damnation. Logan could smell the rain in the air. Around him, cars honked and people busied themselves walking as fast as possible, their eyes fixed somewhere in front of them. He didn't know where he was but he had a faint memory of having just left jail. He turned around but the prison gate wasn't there. His heart raced as the feeling of being lost engulfed him. His hands were fisted. What was he supposed to do now?

His attention was drawn to something he had in his hand. He unclenched it and looked down. He had a bus ticket and a white piece of paper with something written on it. The letters were blurred and he couldn't understand the writing. Where would he go? "Get out of my way, you piece of filth!" someone screamed, bumping into him. Where would he go?

***

Logan blinked his eyes open. His heart was racing and threatened to jump into his throat. He took a deep, ragged breath. Another nightmare. At least this had been a gentle one, unlike the others he'd been having the past couple of months. He sat up in bed and rubbed his eyes. His back was cold and damp. He looked down and realized his skin glistened with sweat, small beads scattered on his abs. Even the elastic band on his boxer shorts was wet. He needed a shower.

Logan pushed the sheets farther away, took a moment to stretch himself and shake that residual dread away and then got up. The feeling of being lost, of not knowing what to do, had been all too real, something he'd gone through as soon as he'd seen himself go free of that jail. There was nothing for him beyond the four walls that had been his only home for five years, no friends or family. The thin thread that had once connected him to his mother had been severed shortly after being put away. She'd never been a great parent and probably thought he wasn't worth the hassle. Logan didn't take it to heart. By then, he was used to her acting like he didn't matter. But he had felt lost with no one waiting for him on the outside. And so, he'd left jail wanting to go back, back to the comfort of the routine he'd known for what seemed like a lifetime. It was fortunate, then, that he'd been forwarded to that shelter. They had been crucial in helping him begin a new life.

Outside his window, summer was now in full force. It was early in the morning and the sun already shining in a deep-blue sky, the trees swayed by a gentle breeze. Logan could tell it would be another hot day. He approached the window and tried to pull it up, but it jammed part way. He needed to tell the landlord. Sooner or later it would get stuck and be impossible to open or close.

As he turned around to go into the bathroom, Buddy entered the bedroom, trotting along cheerfully. He usually spent the night in there, but would get up and go eat something whenever he woke up before Logan, which happened most days.

"Hey, Buddy. Did you sleep well?" Logan asked, crouching and rubbing his hands on each side of Buddy's muzzle. Buddy answered with a short, excited bark. He was always happy. Maybe Logan could learn something from him.

Showering and breakfast took longer than expected and so Logan left the house running. After kissing Buddy goodbye and promising he'd be home sooner this day, he drove off to work. He wasn't late but always enjoyed being the first to arrive. He liked to plan his day before deciding on what to tackle first, and felt it easier when alone.

***

Logan parked the Ford and noticed another vehicle was already there. It looked like Sean Hamilton's car, his other boss who was always traveling the country, searching for the best timber suppliers. Logan had probably seen him three or four times since he'd begun working here. He had this feeling that Mr. Hamilton wasn't one who liked to roll up his sleeves and work the wood, unlike Mr. Shaffer.

He left his truck and went around to the rear entrance. Mr. Hamilton didn't like employees going through the store. Upon entering, he turned on the lights and placed his jacket on its coat hanger, then approached the office door and knocked a couple of times.

"Yes?" a nasal voice said from the other side.

Logan went in. A potato-shaped, middle-aged man stared at him through a frown from behind the desk, making Logan feel uncomfortable for a moment. Then he remembered it was Mr. Hamilton's normal expression. He'd come to realize that the way the skin on his boss' face hung down gave the man a perpetually, almost angry expression.

"Good morning, Mr. Hamilton. I didn't know you were back."

"Yeah, well, someone's got to take care of the bills. This paperwork won't sort itself out."

Logan tried to smile. "If you need me, I'll be in there," he said, pointing at the workshop.

"Before you go, why are those boards so carelessly piled on that assembly table? Did you leave them there like that? They could've slid to the floor overnight. Do you have any idea how much that would've cost me?"

Logan, already leaving, stopped in his tracks, Mr. Hamilton's scold feeling as if someone had poured hot water on him. The boards weren't carelessly piled on the table nor were they in danger of sliding to the floor, either. He knew perfectly well what he was doing, but he'd also learned during his few interactions with his boss not to talk back. It was easier that way. Plus, he knew he shouldn't take it personally. The man seemed to be angry at the world at large.

"It won't happen again, Mr. Hamilton."

"You better make sure it damn well doesn't. Kurt may be happy with you here, but I'm still deciding if you're suitable for my company."

Logan pursed his lips and tried to control his demeanor. "Of course. Can I help you with anything else?"

Mr. Hamilton grunted a "No" while glaring at the stack of papers on his desk, sending Logan away with a wave of his hand. Logan left the office fuming, trying to ignore the man who clearly enjoyed his position of power. Logan had seen him treat other employees like that before, but this had been his first time. It didn't matter what the boss said to him or not, though. He needed the job. His parole evaluation was in a few weeks and he couldn't screw that up. He wouldn't go back to prison again.

Logan spent the morning deep in his work, trying to prove that asshole wrong. He knew perfectly well he'd probably be off back on his trips around the country in no time, but he couldn't help himself. Every time he was treated unfairly, he redoubled his efforts to prove them wrong. There was something about injustice that made his blood boil with an intensity that few things could muster. Probably something that stemmed from being neglected as a kid. He couldn't say for sure. He only knew that it drove him beyond mad.

Around noon, now in the company of his co-workers, the cupboard he'd left on standby the previous day was done. He took a step back and assessed it, looking for flaws. It had none. The assembly was perfect, no visible gaps anywhere and his carved patterns exquisite. Granted, it was a bit too much for his own taste, but the client had insisted. The cupboard had ended up having this old and heavy feel to it that was a far cry from what Logan would've done had the decision been his.

He scratched his forehead and nodded without even realizing he was doing it.

"Hey, Mike," he said to one of the other guys in the workshop, "have you seen Mr. Shaffer?"

"Not since mid-morning."

Logan went in search of the boss he preferred, who'd arrived a couple of hours before in his usual good mood. The order was ready ahead of schedule and Logan wanted to tell him he could call the client to arrange delivery. This was also part of his job and, although he didn't love it, it helped Shaffer & Hamilton Woodworks stand out from the competition. This customized service made the clients feel special, like they had the company's full attention. Not that there were any other shops like theirs in Greenville, the nearest being a good twenty miles away.

He knocked before going into the office but no one answered. Logan opened the door and saw it was empty. He scratched his head, trying to decide if he should go to the front store or wait for his boss to return. It would probably be full of clients browsing the furniture at this time, and Logan felt smelly and self-conscious.

"Ah, screw it," he mumbled to himself. The order was done and he wanted to focus on his next job. He sighed, walked through the office and opened the door into the store. To his surprise, it was virtually empty but for some guy talking to Mr. Shaffer near the entrance. They both had their backs to Logan. The guy was tall, maybe taller than Logan, and so Mr. Shaffer looked awfully short next to him. They were talking while staring at a table but Logan couldn't hear what they were saying. He hesitated and thought of turning to leave, but there was something about the guy that caught his attention. He wore a fitted black T-shirt and dark-blue jeans, a casual outfit that seemed at odds with what regular customers wore. The guy laughed in deep, husky tones that reverberated inside

Logan's chest. Intrigue got the better of him and so he walked on over, noting how the man's broad shoulders contrasted with his slimmer waist. When Logan was an arm's length from the man, he detected a scent of coconut, an invisible, perfumed wall that made him take a deep breath.

Mr. Shaffer turned around at that moment, almost catching Logan with his eyes half-closed, seemingly inebriated by the pleasant odor. The man himself then turned around and Logan immediately felt he'd been punched in the gut. The front view was even dreamier: an attractive square face, short, messy hair and a trimmed beard that extended down to his Adam's apple. Logan's jaw fell, but he snapped his mouth shut just in time.

"I'm... I'm sorry to interrupt, Mr. Shaffer" Logan stammered. "I'll come back another time." Logan had to force himself not to look at the guy, but failed, his eyes forever darting back at him.

"Nonsense. I was just telling Mr. Seddon here about our fine workers." Mr. Shaffer chuckled. "This is Logan Moore, one of our newest craftsmen, but also one of our finest."

The man scanned Logan and smiled. He seemed embarrassed, but Logan had no clue as to why.

"Please, you can call me Kyle," he said in a deep voice, extending his hand.

"Nice to meet you," and Logan shook his hand as the world narrowed down to the man in front of him. "I'm sorry. My hands are all dirty from work," he said, now aware he'd forgotten about all the sawdust and glue.

Kyle smiled. "Don't worry. Nothing that a bit of soap and water can't fix."

Logan smiled back. He felt disturbed by this man who somehow seemed to have the ability to make him sweat and stammer like a school boy caught without an answer. He didn't like it. Such behavior was simply unprofessional.

"So, what did you need me for?" his boss asked.

"Nothing urgent. I just came to say the cupboard's finished and ready to be delivered. But we can talk about it later."

Logan nodded at Kyle and added, "It was very nice meeting you."

"Nice to meet you, too."

Logan smiled one last time and left. He felt the man's gaze burning a hole in his back and willed himself not to look over his shoulder as he walked away.

Chapter Four

Kyle watched Logan walk away. He was still embarrassed by the way his body had reacted to him. For the first time in his life, he felt butterflies in his stomach, something flying around, tickling the inner walls of the gut, bringing a real sense of fear and excitement. His heart had also started pumping hard, and for a moment he'd been afraid the two men could hear it before realizing how silly that was. And then he and Logan had shaken hands and he'd felt shivers run through him, a feverish, electrical storm that had caught him off guard and made his penis twitch. Kyle wanted to know that man better but at the same time felt terrified of the emotional storm Logan had made him go through in just those few short minutes they'd spent together. Was this how it was going to be from now on? Would his blood boil and thicken when presented with a man as attractive as Logan? Kyle wasn't sure he liked it. Maybe he should have kept his feelings buried deep under several layers of denial. It had worked until now.

"…and as you can see, it's not only furniture but a whole range of services we're able to provide in order to—"

"You've convinced me," Kyle said abruptly. The store owner had been talking since Logan left, a buzz in the background that Kyle hadn't really tuned into. "When can you start?"

Mr. Shaffer's grin widened. "I think we can have someone in your house in a couple of days. I just have to check which of my employees I can send over."

Kyle's heart thumped against his ribcage. He didn't want just any of his employees. "How about Logan?" He couldn't believe his own nerve as he said it. His mouth was uttering words almost as if detached from him, giving into some sort of desire he wasn't ready to acknowledge.

Mr. Shaffer unfocused his eyes and scratched the back of his head. "I guess. He's just finished a job… Let me check my appointment book and I'll get back to you as soon as possible. Would that be okay?"

Kyle was mortified but also excited, all at the same time. He couldn't explain the glee he'd felt upon seeing Logan or why he was behaving this way. It was as if there were two of him inside his head, an overexcited and curious teenager who had no concern for the rules, who just wanted to make up for all those years lost; and the more mature and cautious self, grumbling about how this wasn't the proper way for a grown man to behave. Right now, though, the teenager in him was winning and he wasn't sure he liked it. Sure, Logan had rugged good looks and strong, rough hands; his body seemed toned from working in a demanding job and his deep-brown eyes made Kyle's knees weak, but he didn't even know the guy. He should be thinking of his son, Ryan, instead of some casual flirt.

"Of course. Forgive me for intruding. Please, take your time and call me later," Kyle said, forcing his lips to curve into a gentle smile. They shook hands and Kyle left the store.

Ryan had been the reason he'd summoned up the courage to be honest with himself in the first place. He didn't want his son to grow up in a broken home next to a father who was always angry at everyone and everything just because he hadn't had the courage to be himself. But at the same time he felt utterly selfish for embarking on a journey of self-discovery and leaving his son with his mother, even if it was for a good cause. Most of all, he feared he'd be missing out on all the little things toddlers did. Every day was replete with discoveries and adventures, and up until now Kyle had been there to be a part of them. He only hoped Ryan wouldn't forget him.

Kyle scoffed. "You're being overly dramatic," he said to himself, then shook his head and made his way to the grocery store. His pantry was still empty and he couldn't continue coming downtown every time his stomach grumbled about being hungry.

His phone rang when he was about to enter the store. He didn't recognize the number but answered it anyway.

"Hello?"

"Hi, Kyle? It's Eric Penn."

Kyle cringed. Eric was a client who'd commissioned a work a couple of weeks before. They usually talked over e-mail so Kyle hadn't gotten around to saving the man's phone number.

"Hey, Eric. How are you?" He probably wanted an update on his project, something Kyle really couldn't do right now as his laptop was back at the house. Besides, he hadn't worked on the job for almost a week.

"Good, good. I sent you an email this morning and was wondering if you got it."

"You did? Oh, I'm sorry. My Internet has been down all morning and I haven't read any emails." Kyle didn't like to lie but he also couldn't explain that he was going through a separation because at twenty-seven he'd decided he was gay after all.

Eric chuckled. "I figured something was wrong. That's why I called. Can you give me an update on the logo? Are we still on track for the deadline? I'd like to order the new business cards as soon as possible, as I'm traveling abroad soon."

Kyle cringed again and pinched the bridge of his nose. "Sure thing. I've been sketching some ideas and I think next week I can show you two or three options."

"That's definitely good news," Eric's voice chirped through the earpiece. "Maybe we can video chat about it as soon as I receive your proposals. I think it's easier and faster that way."

Kyle agreed and hung up. Being a graphic designer was one of the reasons he'd decided to move to Greenville. He already worked from home anyway, so it didn't really matter where that home was. Now he only had to work on his self-discipline, forget about his family problems and ignore the fact that his new house was far from being a place to feel inspired. Easy-peasy.

He went into the store, the few heads in there turning around to look at him. Kyle smiled and nodded, after which he picked up a basket and headed to find the produce aisle. Since arriving in town, the amount of attention he seemed to draw everywhere he went made him a bit uncomfortable. In the city, nobody knew him and nobody cared. Kyle was beginning to think that coming to a small town to start over might not have been his best decision. At the time, though, it had made perfect sense. Greenville was close enough to Ryan's mother that he could drop by easily, and as his grandmother had left him the house in her will, he didn't have to pay rent. Being there was much nicer than moving into a minuscule apartment in the city, for which he'd have to pay an indecent amount of money.

Kyle tried to clear his mind of everything as he observed the fruit aisle. He felt like eating a nice salad but couldn't find avocados anywhere. Maybe they had them in the vegetables section?

"Excuse me," he said to a lady who was placing a couple of oranges into her basket, "do you know if they sell avocados?"

She turned to him, all smiles. She appeared to be in her fifties, but he couldn't really tell for sure as she dressed like she was ninety. Her clothes were all made from heavy fabrics despite the temperature outside hovering around eighty-five degrees. Just looking at her made Kyle sweat.

"Hmm. Avocados?" She scanned the fruit and turned again to Kyle. "I really don't know. I'm sorry. Have you tried the vegetables section?" She frowned but then smiled, before adding, "I guess I've never bought avocados before."

She laughed and Kyle smiled. "You should try them. They're very tasty in salads."

"They are? Fruit in a salad. I'd never thought of that." She stared at a point somewhere next to Kyle when she spoke, but her eyes focused on him again as she tilted her head slightly. "I don't think I've seen you around here before. I'm Beth."

"Nice to meet you. I'm Kyle. I arrived yesterday," he said, shaking her hand.

"Ah, fresh out of town, then. What's brought you here? Nature?"

Kyle chuckled. "Actually, I moved in. I traded the big city for a quiet, small town. I'm hoping it's a nice place to live in."

"You'll love it here, you'll see. And you seem like an honest young man, exactly the kind of people we need around here. The good Lord doesn't take dishonesty too kindly." She grinned a bit more, and added: "Do you have any children?"

"A two-year-old boy. Well, he's almost two."

Beth giggled, which made Kyle uncomfortable. There was something in that laughter that left him wondering about her. He fidgeted and tried to smile.

"Ah, I bet your boy is a handful. Boys that age always are, bless them. You should bring him and your wife to our church. The building's a modest one but the congregation is very welcoming. I can show you how to get there if you like."

Kyle pursed his lips. The more Beth spoke, the more uncomfortable he felt. He really didn't want to lie but he'd no intention of explaining himself to a complete stranger, even if she looked like someone else's grandmother.

"Thanks, but we're not really churchgoers." He wanted to leave but didn't know how to without seeming rude.

"Maybe I can change your mind. It's never too late to embrace our Lord's teachings."

"Some other time, maybe." Kyle smiled and motioned to leave the aisle. Beth said goodbye and waved like they were longtime friends. Kyle nodded and tried to shake off an aggravation that had come out of nowhere.

He arrived at the vegetables section still fuming but not quite sure why he felt so upset. He was beginning to think he probably wasn't ready to be out and proud, as they said. Maybe that shame about himself was what had made him angry at that poor lady. He put those thoughts aside while searching for what he'd come in here for. He'd deal with them later, both them and that image of Logan that had been burned into his mind, of the one who made his blood thick every time he thought about him.

Chapter Five

Logan got out of his truck and was immediately blanketed by the oppressive heat. The late-morning high temperatures made him wish he was inside a tub of cold water. It had been easier to bear them inside the Ford, but only slightly and only while driving.

The house now in front of him seemed weathered down, as though it hadn't been used in a while. Around it, the property extended for a couple of miles of verdant countryside, nothing but trees and footpaths to explore. Logan wasn't too familiar with this part of the county but was almost sure the same creek that flowed near his own house passed around here as well.

He turned to face the house again and sighed. You got this. You're a professional and you're gonna act like one. He made his way to the front door, unsure why he was so nervous. Mr. Shaffer had decided that Logan would be working with their new client, Kyle, as the man had asked specifically for him. Logan had been taken aback, a mix of surprise and excitement taking him over, without knowing exactly why he felt like it or where these feelings were coming from. Mr. Shaffer didn't know why Kyle had asked for him, exactly, only that he'd probably made a good first impression. So, here Logan was, ready to be as professional as possible but still trying to control his emotions. He couldn't let this new client realize how he really felt.

Logan stopped before the door and tried to quell his gut. There was no reason to be this nervous. What, the guy was cute? Was that it? He had had his fair share of handsome guys in the past and that alone wasn't reason to be this electrified. Granted, at first sight Kyle seemed like a sweet guy, and the mix of good looks and shyness gave him a special appeal. Logan thought again of their handshake the previous day and his skin gathered in goosebumps. He could think of a million reasons not to engage in those kinds of thoughts but there was really only one that mattered: Kyle was a client and he couldn't risk losing him. Mr. Shaffer would certainly not be happy if that happened and it would stain an otherwise spotless record since he'd begun working for him.

He knocked and waited. A moment later, he heard footsteps approaching from within. Logan held his breath when the door opened. Before him now was a sweaty Kyle in a tank top, revealing strong arms and a large chest. The fabric was glued to his torso and Logan could see hints of his sinewy build beneath it.

"Hi, I'm Logan. From Shaffer & Hamilton Woodworks? We met yesterday," Logan was able to say, despite himself.

"Hi. Of course. I remember you. I'm sorry for answering the door looking like this," Kyle said, looking down and moving his arms away from his chest, a slight grimace twisting his charming demeanor, "but I've been cleaning my house like a crazy person and there's no air conditioning. I really need to shower again." He chuckled, sounding apologetic, as if sweating was something alien that normal people were immune to, even after strenuous exercise.

"I know what you mean. I sometimes shower twice in the same day. It's this damn heat," Logan chuckled and tried to ignore the man's frame and his chiseled lines. He'd gawped unwillingly at Kyle a moment before but hoped he hadn't noticed.

"Please, come in...and don't mind the mess," Kyle said, making way for Logan.

From the entrance hall, Logan could see the stairs to the upper floor and a living room to his left that appeared to have only the bare essentials. There was a light breeze running through the house, which made the temperature inside ever so slightly more bearable. Even so, there was a stale smell in the air mixed with something akin to bleach, like the house had been closed for a very long time and was now under heavy scrubbing.

"Please, follow me," and Kyle led Logan to the stairs.

They creaked under their weight as they went up. Logan glanced at Kyle's ass, now popping beautifully under his jeans, but quickly looked away. It would be much easier to be professional if he stopped ogling the guy.

"This is it," Kyle said a moment later, stopping and propping his hands on his hips.

Logan looked around. They were in an empty room, apart from a built-in closet. He offloaded his tool bag from his shoulder, placed it on the floor and grabbed a small notepad where he'd jotted down Kyle's requirements before driving over.

"So, if I understand correctly, you need a bed, a nightstand and a desk. You didn't tell Mr. Shaffer its size, though." Logan looked up at Kyle and added: "But judging by your size, I'd say you need a king-size."

Kyle blushed and Logan's insides melted.

"Maybe I didn't explain myself correctly. This bedroom isn't for me. It's for my son. And the desk is actually a changing dresser. You know, for diapers and stuff."

Logan's insides froze solid. "Oh, you have a son?" He tried to sound casual but felt like someone had punched him in his gut. Knowing that Kyle was married with kids meant the end to his little fantasy. He'd tried to read Kyle the day before in the shop but hadn't been able to figure out if he was gay or not. This settled it.

"My little man's almost two years old," he said, smiling from ear to ear. "So I guess a king-sized bed would be overkill."

Cute and with a sense of humor. Now, that was a deadly combination. It was such a shame he was straight and unavailable.

"I guess you're right," Logan said, chuckling, trying to ignore the gaping hole that had just opened up inside him. He squatted and rummaged through his tool bag, looking for his laser measuring tape. It was good to know the size of a room before starting to work on a new order. It helped him gain a better feel for the correct size of the furniture. Sometimes, clients would ask for a piece that was clearly too big for the space they had. Generally, people had a terrible idea of the real size of things. After getting up again, Logan moved to a wall, against which he firmly placed the gadget. Kyle watched him with a puzzled expression.

"I'm sorry, but would you mind taking a step back so I can measure this distance?"

Kyle complied. "Is that one of those laser-measuring tools?"

Logan nodded, impressed that Kyle would know such a thing.

Kyle let out a short laugh and shook his head. "That's so cool! I've seen them online but I've never been this close to one. Can you show me how it works?"

Before Logan could answer, Kyle was already by his side, taking turns in staring at him and his contraption. Logan could feel the man's body heat and smell his musky aroma, a mix of sweat and deodorant that wafted into his nose, that spread through his lungs and signaled his penis to spring into action.

"Erm… Sure. I just place this on the wall and press this button. It can even tell me square footage in the end if I want."

"So awesome! I'm sorry, you must think I'm crazy or something, but I've always been a gadget freak, and that definitely falls into my category of awesome ones."

Kyle's enthusiasm was almost palpable. His wide grin definitely showed how excited he was about the tool, almost as if he were a kid looking for the first time at a strange, new toy. Their eyes met but Logan quickly looked away. He took a step back and, still smiling, went to another wall to take a further measurement. The physical effect Kyle had on him left him embarrassed and mad at himself. Kyle was married and had a kid. There was nothing here for him.

"So, what brings you to Greenville?" he asked, trying to make small talk and ignore his galloping heart.

Kyle's demeanor changed from one of enthusiasm to one of sadness. After hesitating for a moment, he finally said, "I'm getting divorced from my wife." He said it in a blunt, dry way, like he had to get it out of his chest in one go or he wouldn't be able to. "And as this house is mine, it seemed like a good idea to move up here until the dust settles."

Logan felt his face heating up. Great way of changing the subject! "I'm sorry. I didn't mean to pry."

"That's okay. You had no way of knowing."

"Well, it sure looks like a great house to start over." Logan paused while looking around. "If you don't mind my asking, what do you do for a living?" Logan was again trying to make small talk but it still felt inappropriate.

"I'm a freelance graphic designer."

Logan took a deep breath. His question may have been unprofessional, but at least Kyle didn't seem to notice. "Seems like a fancy line of work."

Kyle chuckled. "It's not. Trust me. Most of the time it involves me on the phone with a client, or skyping with them, trying to summon up a miracle and arguing minute details."

"Sounds like what I do. Well, minus the skyping and the minute details with clients. That's normally Mr. Shaffer's work."

"Let's just hope I don't turn into a difficult client for you, then." Kyle scratched his beard. He seemed to be thinking of something. Then, smiling, he approached Logan. "In fact, I'll tell you this: I promise not to turn into one of those difficult clients, but if I do, promise you'll tell me immediately. Deal?" Kyle extended his hand.

"Deal," Logan said, smiling as he shook it, Kyle's musky odor titillating Logan's brain again.

"Great! What do you say we seal the deal with a couple of beers?"

Kyle was already at the door, ready to go downstairs. His cheerfulness was beginning to cloud Logan's better judgement.

"I shouldn't. I'm working." Kyle's happy demeanor began to melt away and so did Logan's resolve. "But if you promise not to tell on me, I don't see why I can't have one."

"You've got yourself a deal."

Chapter Six

Kyle jumped the two last steps and landed on the floor with a thud. He had to control this giddiness he felt for having Logan here. What would the guy think? They'd barely met and he was already acting like they were best buds, making him promise things and offering him beer. As he entered the kitchen, a draft made its way through an open window and swirled around the room, making him suddenly very aware of his own body odor. He grimaced as his nose was drowned in what was clearly the smell of sweat. Oh dear lord! He smelled! And Logan had probably noticed it, too. Of course he had. How could he not, especially when Kyle had been all over him, asking questions about that silly laser contraption? He squeezed his arms against his torso in a futile attempt to keep his armpit odor in check. Of course he knew he was sweaty but he hadn't realized he smelled. What should he do? Go shower before returning with the beers? No, probably not. He couldn't possibly justify disappearing for five or ten minutes just to take a shower. Could he?

He sighed and went to the fridge. Why was he so worried about smelling, anyway? He'd been working his ass off cleaning the house so it was only natural. Plus, Logan was probably used to it since he worked in carpentry, right? He cringed, opened the fridge and took out two beers, wondering if what he was experiencing was a crush or not. Up until deciding to be honest with himself, and face all the excuses he'd been coming up with throughout his life, Kyle had always brushed off his interest in men as a byproduct of that natural curiosity everyone had for their own gender. Back then, his two minds had already been struggling with each other, he realized that now: one whispering to him that a guy was cute while the other rushed to explain that he wasn't, per se, but that his chiseled features gave him a classical beauty that anyone could appreciate, man or woman. These two wills would often perform intricate choreographies inside his mind, making him ogle discretely at guys in the locker room while trying to rationalize it with some sort of half-baked excuse. Kyle usually ended up concluding that all he'd wanted to do was see how their bodies looked, so he could mimic them when working out. Up until recently, his feelings had been concealed beneath a blur of denial and delusional explanations, all meant to hide the fact he was gay and that he wasn't in love with his wife. What killed him, though, was realizing that he did love her, he really did, just not as much as he wanted to. It gutted him to know his actions had hurt her in a way he'd never hurt anyone before. But that talk with Jessica had been inevitable. His sanity had depended on it, as he'd found out when, one day, he'd found himself contemplating crashing his car into a tree, as though that was somehow something normal, something that would bring him instant relief and shut out his true desires once and for all.

So, no, Kyle didn't know if he was nervous around Logan because he had a crush on him or just because he was a hot guy and on some level he wanted to be with him. The only thing he knew for sure was that he smelled and was deeply embarrassed by it.

When he arrived in the bedroom, Logan was writing something down in his notebook. In his large hands, that notebook seemed smaller than he knew it was. Kyle forced himself not to look but his eyes landed on Logan's T-shirt, the sleeves straining to contain his bulging arms. He could see Logan's well-defined muscles contracting as he jotted down this and that. Damn, the man's frame sure was big and strong.

Kyle ended up scanning his chiseled face, trying to guess his age. In a way, Logan seemed ageless, young and mature, all at the same time.

Kyle sighed and approached him. "Here," he said, "the beers aren't ice cold, but they're cold enough. I think the fridge has been having a hard time fighting this heat." As soon as Logan took the beer, Kyle stepped back and leaned against the doorway.

"Thanks." Logan took a swig. "Ah, that was good. This damn heat is killing me." He then cooled his forehead against the bottle. Kyle smiled and wished he could be as carefree as Logan seemed to be.

"How do people get used to it, anyway?"

Logan gazed at Kyle for a moment and then shrugged. "I don't know. I guess folks here go to the lake, but I'm yet to go there myself."

"You're not from around here?"

Logan seemed to freeze for a moment, the bottle against his lips. He shook his head. "I moved here about six months ago. My house is actually about four miles from yours, up in that direction." He pointed somewhere behind Kyle, not really sure exactly which way it was. His sense of direction had never been good.

"Maybe we could hang out one of these days. I don't really know anyone around here and could use a friend to show me where to have a drink or a good meal," but then Kyle blushed. He'd heard himself speaking, but as though eavesdropping on someone else. Before he knew it, he was blabbering on about being friends and going out for drinks. Embarrassment engulfed him despite it all sounding pretty innocent. After all, he wasn't lying or concocting some sort of scheme. He really could use a friend.

Logan blinked at Kyle a couple of times and opened his mouth but no sound came out. Then, after a moment, he said, "Sure. I also don't really know anyone around here. Everyone's either married or too old. Not that being old's a problem. It's just harder to have something in common." Logan pursed his lips. Kyle had the feeling he was going to say something else but Logan only placed his beer on the floor near the wall and took a catalogue from his bag. "I'm leaving this here with you. Give it a look and see what kind of furniture you want for your kid. When you're ready, just give us a call."

Kyle took the catalogue Logan handed him and watched as he put his laser gadget back into the bag and closed it.

"You're leaving?"

"I have to head back to work. Thanks for the beer, though."

For a microsecond Logan didn't appear to know what to do, to shake Kyle's hand or just leave, but after an awkward dance with his arms he finally extend his hand.

Kyle shook it and said, "I'll walk you to the door."

They both went downstairs in silence, the wood creaking under their feet seemingly amplified by it. Kyle went ahead and opened the door for Logan, who nodded and said goodbye. Kyle watched him walk to his pickup truck and noticed how his jeans hugged his ass in a way that made it pop. He also realized he was getting hard.

Kyle raised his hand for a final goodbye as Logan arrived at his truck and got in, a wave of embarrassment and excitement washing over him. Had Logan seen his bulge twitching? Don't be ridiculous. It's not that big. Kyle panted as his heart rapped against his ribcage. A silky silence surrounded him, making him terribly aware of himself and his thoughts towards Logan. He couldn't explain why his body was acting this way. He only knew he wanted to see Logan again, to be near him. Maybe even to have the courage to…to kiss him.

The thought got Kyle's heart to jumping again and his legs faltered. His body was reacting in ways that reminded him of his early teens, when he'd first experienced an orgasm. It was all so intense, so new, so impossible to control. Logan was probably his first real crush since he'd been honest with himself. He'd had other men-crushes, but he'd never openly thought about them. At least, not in this way. But now, he told himself, he wasn't constrained by his own shackles. With a smile on his lips, he came to the conclusion that from now on he was free to explore his desires.

Chapter Seven

Logan cranked the window open as he drove back to town. He needed to breathe and to think but the warm air blowing on his face was not helping him cool down. Had he and Kyle shared a moment back there? Did he imagine it? Logan didn't really know but hoped the moment had been real; hoped and feared, all at the same time. He couldn't stop thinking of Kyle since he'd set foot in the shop with his charming good looks and sturdy frame. But beyond being a handsome man, there was also kindness in his dark-brown eyes, something that immediately appealed to Logan and made Kyle so much more attractive.

For all his charming good looks, though, Logan feared Kyle wouldn't react well if he ever found out he was an ex-convict. Those days as a thief were over and nothing now but a distant memory, one he wanted to forget and bury. Despite his efforts at being a different man, the truth was that most people couldn't see beyond his criminal record. Logan's first weeks out of jail had been terrible. The few job interviews he'd gone to all ended with empty promises of getting back to him. He knew it, they knew it, but they all danced around the truth like civilized people. Logan could see the judgement in their eyes and the subtle changes in their demeanor. It made him lose all hope of ever being able to overcome his past, but then the shelter had helped him get a job far away from there, in a whole new town. The owners were more than happy to welcome him into their company and give Logan an opportunity for a fresh start. It had felt like a miracle at the time, and although he couldn't imagine why anyone in some distant town would give him such a chance, he'd taken it without looking back. Logan later found out that Mr. Shaffer had been involved in a car accident and had almost died. Since then, he'd become a different person and was always trying to help others. Logan also found out that Sean Hamilton, the other partner, wasn't too thrilled about having him there.

None of that mattered now. What mattered was how Kyle would react if he knew. He seemed a kind, good guy, so maybe he'd be different.

"Why in the hell are you even thinking about this? The guy's married. He's got a kid, for crying out loud!"

Logan was loud enough to make himself heard above the engine noise. Talking alone was for crazy people, but it had been a way to keep his mind sane in prison. And anyway, that was a very good question. Why was he weighing the pros and cons of telling Kyle he'd been in jail? He was a straight man who just wanted a friend to have a few drinks with. But that moment he thought they'd had in his house? Probably nothing but wishful thinking brought on by his loneliness, a loneliness he'd felt for so long. Before going to jail he'd had a few flings here and there and one-night stands. He had never allowed himself to feel anything more than a sexual interest in those men, though. His life hadn't been fit to think about building a future with someone, so he'd never let himself. But that had been in another lifetime. Now, things were different and it was only natural for him to want to have a connection with a cute guy like Kyle, even if he was straight. At least it would be a departure from fending off the sexual advances of the town's cougars.

He parked the truck and went into Shaffer & Hamilton Woodworks ready to forget about the whole Kyle thing. He should focus on his job, not some fantasy with a straight guy. His parole officer would be contacting him soon to assess him, and the last thing he wanted was to be out of a job by then. He couldn't risk it. His freedom was at stake.

"Back so soon?" Mr. Shaffer asked after seeing Logan enter the workshop. He liked to be there with his employees when things were slow in the store.

Logan focused on the world around him and saw Mr. Shaffer smiling and waiting for his answer. "Yeah. Turns out there was a misunderstanding."

"Oh?"

"The furniture is for his son, not him. I measured the bedroom and left Ky…Mr. Seddon a catalogue, so he can chose the style of furniture he wants."

"For a moment there I thought you were going to say he didn't want our services anymore." Mr. Shaffer chuckled and Logan did the same. "Well, it's almost time for my lunch break," he said looking at his wristwatch, "but I'd like to have a word with you before that. Can you step into my office?"

Logan held his breath. His work colleagues glanced discreetly both at him and Mr. Shaffer. Was he in trouble? He couldn't think of anything he'd done wrong. He tried to smile. "Sure thing, Mr. Shaffer."

His boss opened the office door for Logan and he went in, Mr. Shaffer following him, closing the door behind them. The workshop was cooler than the street outside, where the inclement sun was cooking everything to a brown crisp. But the small office was even cooler, an air conditioning unit right above their heads pumping out cold air. The shock made Logan's skin gather into goosebumps.

Mr. Shaffer sat behind his desk. "Sit."

Logan smiled and complied. His mind was racing, trying to find the moment when he'd screwed everything, the reason why his boss had asked him in here. What was he going to do? How was he going to explain this to his parole officer?

Mr. Shaffer gave Logan a good, long look, after which he said, "You've been with us for six months now, isn't that right?"

He was smiling. That was a good sign, right?

"Yes, Mr. Shaffer. Six months and almost two weeks."

"And how do you like it here? And please, be honest. I don't want any of that pleasing crap everyone thinks they're required to say when their boss asks them a question."

"I like it here very much. I love what I do, the guys are nice, it pays well... So, yeah, all in all I'd say I'm happy to be here and working for you." It was all true. Logan wasn't sugarcoating it.

"Do you think you'd be prepared for a bit more responsibility, then?"

Logan blinked. "What do you mean?"

Mr. Shaffer's gaze zoomed in on Logan. "I like to think everyone deserves a chance, even if society thinks otherwise. I don't care about what other people might think. That's why you're here with us. And despite Sean's grumpy remarks, please know that we're both very pleased with you and your work. He just says the things he says because he still thinks people will only respect him if he treats them like small children." His boss chuckled, the chair creaking under his weight. "You're always on time, you're responsible—a bit of a perfectionist, even— and I've never seen you leave with work to be done. And to be honest, I like the way you understand our clients' needs and translate that into pieces of furniture, although I'm perfectly aware that dealing with them is not your favorite part of the work."

"Thank you, Mr. Shaffer."

The man smiled. "Anyhow, I also think people grow best if they're given a chance at it. That's why I want you to start being responsible for your own projects, starting with this new one at Mr. Seddon's. You'll be solely responsible for every decision needed to finish the work, from start to finish. It's a small job and I think it's the best way to start you on this new chapter."

Logan's jaw fell. He wasn't expecting this. He was being...being promoted?

"Thanks, Mr. Shaffer. I... I'm more than happy to accept this added responsibility." Logan's wide grin reflected how proud he felt. He knew the other guys were normally responsible for entire projects and would sometimes recruit the others to help with them, should the need arise. He'd never thought he'd be at that same level, though; the same level as them.

"And don't worry. This also means a pay raise. I'm not trying to exploit you." Mr. Shaffer chuckled. "I'll let Martha fine tune the details with you. Now, scoot. I have a meeting with a hot sandwich."

"Thanks, Mr. Shaffer. I appreciate it, I really do." Logan got up from the chair and was about to leave, his hand already on the door handle, when he realized he had nothing to do until Kyle called. "Mr. Shaffer," he said as he turned to him, "I don't have anything to do right now. Should I go help one of the guys?"

His boss was already head-deep in the mini-fridge he kept next to his desk. He looked over his shoulder. "Don't be silly. Those guys are more than able to handle their work. You can go home early if you want to celebrate. Or work in your personal projects."

"Thanks, Mr. Shaffer."

Logan left the office with a balloon-like feeling inside his chest, his steps so light he felt he could jump and reach the sky. For the first time in his life he felt appreciated. Someone was rewarding him for his hard work and for being good at it, and it was thrilling. It made him feel like a complete person.

He arrived at his pickup-truck with a wide grin on his face, trying to decide what to do next. It was almost lunchtime, the sun high and hot in the sky and Logan was beginning to sweat. The chat he'd had with Kyle about what people did around here popped into his mind and he found himself thinking about the lake. He'd seen it from a distance but hadn't gone there yet. He closed the truck's door and headed to the store to buy some sandwiches and beer. He and Buddy would take a trip to the lake and enjoy a bit of cool air for a change. The thought of calling Kyle and inviting him to go with him crossed his mind but he decided against it. He'd gone over this already. He wasn't going to jeopardize losing Kyle as a client, especially now he'd been promoted.

"Excuse me, young man. Could I have a minute of your time?"

A woman dressed in heavy garments stood in the shadow of a tree, behind a small table, a clipboard in her hand as she gave him a most pleasant smile. Next to her stood a man wearing a short-sleeved shirt and a pair of khaki pants. His drooping eyes gave him a tired expression; or an angry one—Logan couldn't decide. On the table were a couple of pens and a small stack of pamphlets, the writing too small for him to read.

Logan smiled and approached her out of politeness.

"Hello," he said with the feeling he'd seen her before.

"Thank you so much, dear. I need your help with something disgraceful. We're collecting signatures because our family values are being threatened by a group of people who think they can defy our Good Lord. We want to help our county clerks fight this offensive ruling that forces them against their will to marry certain people. It's tarnishing the good name of the sanctity of holy matrimony and forcing people to go against their beliefs."

The woman was smiling but her words were wrapped up in contempt and anger. Logan frowned as the acidity of her words began to corrode the bubbly feelings he'd left the workshop with.

"I'm sorry, but I'm not sure I'm following you…"

"We just want the Governor to issue a bill exempting our clerks from marrying the homosexuals. People shouldn't be forced to do the bidding of the perverts that have taken a hold of this country. Marriage is a holy bond between a man and a woman, and we shouldn't be forced to act against the will of God."

Logan's face flared with anger. His jaw welded shut, though, as he tried not to say something he'd later regret. "Well, that doesn't make any sense. Marrying gays has nothing to do with God. It's something the State is doing, not a priest. And as far as I know, State and Church are separated in this country, aren't they? So why should a clerk collect his paycheck if he doesn't want to do his job?" He regretted asking the question immediately. He didn't want to know. He just wanted to leave and be done with people like her. But his mouth was working against his better judgement.

The woman still sported a smile on her lips but her eyes narrowed down to two slits. "Our good Lord has ruled that sodomy is a sin, and that should be enough. It's unnatural what those people do and we shouldn't have to stand it. We can't stand it. If it's against nature, it's against God's plan and all that's good. Do you want to live in a country that promotes evil? Their lifestyle?"

Logan felt sick to his stomach. Clearly, the woman felt so morally superior she failed to see how she was spreading intolerance, contradicting the very commandments of love and understanding she supposedly adhered to. Logan never understood what drove people like her to spread so much hate. As far as he knew, religion taught people to be good, kind and loving, right? Alas, this woman was the exact opposite.

"Again, this country isn't ruled by the church. And that's a good thing because as far as I know people aren't very happy in the Middle East, or for that matter every other place where the church meddles with their everyday lives. I'm happy the Spanish Inquisition isn't a thing anymore. So, no, I'm not gonna sign your petition. I don't believe in spreading hate. It's wrong and you should be ashamed of yourself for doing so. Go read a Bible for real because I think you've skipped the part that says not to judge people and to love them instead."

The woman opened her mouth to speak but Logan had already turned his back on her. His temples were now thumping and his heart galloping. He was furious about her lack of empathy and compassion. He headed to the grocery store and tried to forget about the hag. He wouldn't let her ruin his day. After all, he'd just been promoted. That was all that mattered.

Chapter Eight

It had been a good day. Logan had managed to forget about the horrible encounter with the preachy woman as soon as Buddy met him at home with his usual dose of high energy and affection. Buddy always seemed to guess when Logan was feeling down. He met him with happy barks, a wagging tail and an extra dose of licking. It was disgusting but Logan loved it.

Their afternoon by the lake turned out to be wonderful. The lake was much bigger than Logan had expected and its peaceful waters made the air much cooler on the shoreline. The trees covered the hills all the way down to its shore, so it wasn't hard choosing between basking in the sun and seeking refuge in the shade when the heat became unbearable. Logan had never seen Buddy this excited. After arriving, he barked suspiciously at the water, assuming that low stance he always took before something new. As soon as Logan dove in, though, Buddy did the same and spent the next couple of hours swimming with an excited look in his eyes, coming ashore from time to time to shake the water off and sprinkle everything around him. After that he'd bark excitedly at Logan before going back in.

They returned home well after eight. The sun was still high in the sky and the air plenty warm, but the light already had that faded tone that preceded nightfall. Even so, Logan was convinced it was still the middle of the afternoon. That unexpected break from work during a weekday had left his mind kind of jetlagged. And the light meal he'd eaten by the lake just reinforced his feeling that it was still quite early.

Soon after they arrived home, Buddy went to the living room to take a nap. Although Logan felt tired too, it was way too early even to think of going to sleep. Instead, he went to the garage where he had set up a little workspace for his projects. His latest was a swing bench he intended installing on his porch. He liked to be there at night, observing the stars, and a porch swing would make the whole experience much cozier.

The air inside the garage was thick and the temperature a bit too hot to be comfortable. Logan opened the outer door and drew in a deep breath as the slightly cooler breeze made its way in. He turned back to the table he'd set up to work on. On the counter was a stack of boards that needed cutting. He had already measured them, so now they only needed sawing. Logan didn't care very much for power tools, preferring to do it the old-fashioned way with a handsaw. The manual work made him feel good and there was nothing more rewarding than having his arms aching after a good stretch of work.

He grabbed the first board and secured it in the vise. Then he proceeded to saw it, which only took a couple of minutes. The fir he'd gotten for the bench wasn't the hardest of lumbers, but the boards had to be thick enough to carry a grown man's weight. He finished the first and cleaned the sweat from his forehead with the back of his hand. One board down, fourteen more to go, he thought. He took his shirt off before resuming work and tossed it onto the counter. It was getting glued to him and not helping at all with his sawing.

Half an hour later and Logan was done. He was dripping sweat and somewhat tired, but happy with the result. He stacked the lumber behind him and was about to call it a day when he heard a car approaching. He turned to his garage door and saw the headlights of a dark-grey SUV pulling up on his driveway.

Logan headed outside as it came to a stop. It was getting dark but the daylight was still enough to see who was inside.

Kyle.

Logan cleaned his hands on his jeans and approached the SUV, wondering what Kyle was doing here. He was thrilled to see him but tried his hardest to contain his excitement. He was only a couple of steps away from the car when he realized he was bare-chested and probably looked completely disgusting. He winced mentally but it was too late to do anything about it.

Kyle stepped out of the car, his lips pursed and a weird look in his eyes. Maybe he thought Logan was some hillbilly for being half-naked and all sweaty.

"Hey, Logan. I'm sorry for dropping by unannounced. You're obviously busy…" and he briefly pointed at him.

Logan looked down before locking eyes with Kyle. "I was working in my garage." There was an awkward pause when neither of them seemed to know what to say. "What can I do for you? Have you decided on the furniture you want?" Logan felt annoyed at the idea that Kyle was here to talk about work.

"Oh, no, no. I was driving around and thought I could try and find your place. I did and here I am." Kyle smiled awkwardly before adding, "I was thinking we could go for a beer, like we talked about earlier." He licked his lips. "Maybe I should've called you before coming here, but you said your house was close to mine and so I thought I could give it a try. I'm sorry. I'll go."

Logan was surprised and confused. Straight guys didn't drive out at night to meet men they barely knew just to ask them to go for a drink. Did they? He scanned Kyle more attentively but his gaydar was still confused. Maybe he was just bored and alone, and really was just looking for a friend. Suddenly, Logan felt completely naked.

"Nonsense. I'm glad you dropped by. I could use a beer right now but I have to take a quick shower first."

"Oh, great," Kyle said, sounding relieved.

"Come in. I'll be ready in five. Do you want something to drink? Oh, and by the way, I have a dog, but don't worry about him, he's friendly. You're not afraid of dogs, are you?"

"No, I love them."

Inside the house, Logan heard Buddy woofing in the living room as soon as they crossed the threshold and then his claws clicking on the wooden floors as he approached.

"Buddy, we have a guest," he said, crouching and petting the dog's head.

Buddy wagged his tail while gazing up at Logan, then focused his attention on Kyle and barked a couple of times. Logan could hear it was his friendly bark, but Kyle seemed uneasy.

"He's just welcoming you. Don't worry," he said, looking at Kyle.

"I'm not sure he likes me."

Logan wanted to say that that was impossible because he was adorable. Instead, he just said, "Let him sniff your hand. You'll see he just wants to meet you."

Kyle nodded and leaned towards Buddy, placing his hand close to the dog's snout. Buddy sniffed it a couple of times, then proceeded to lick it.

"I told you he liked you."

Kyle chuckled. "I guess he does."

"I'll leave you two to get to know each other better. I'll be right back." Logan showed Kyle to the living room and Buddy followed them. After making sure Kyle was comfortable, Logan went upstairs while Kyle tried to fend off Buddy's advances, who by now was trying to jump onto his lap and lick his face.

Logan tried not to run to the bathroom. He didn't want Kyle to notice how excited he was. Still, he walked as fast as he could without making too much noise. He felt nervous about Kyle being here and wanted to scrub off the sweat and body odor. In his haste to get into the shower, he ended up entangling himself in his own jeans and falling to the floor, banging his knees. Now in pain and with his bare ass pointing at the ceiling, he felt pretty embarrassed with himself.

"Stupid, stupid, stupid."

Finally in the shower, he had a quick scrub before finding himself back in his bedroom, feeling much lighter and clean.

His knee still hurt but he chose to ignore it. He quickly put on a fresh pair of jeans and a T-shirt, and after sliding into his sneakers, strode downstairs, his heart beating a little faster than could be excused by the exercise of having a shower. He also needed to tame the grin that insisted on spreading across his lips.

Right before going into the living room, Logan put his hand in his front pocket to make sure he had his keys with him and realized he'd completely forgotten to put on his boxer shorts. His penis was hanging-out with his left leg like they were best pals, brushing together at every step. Logan groaned. How could he have forgotten about something so simple? He wondered about going back upstairs, but Kyle had already seen him and was getting up from the couch. Logan just hoped his penis wouldn't be too visible, especially as he couldn't decide if its greater freedom was making him uncomfortable or aroused.

"Is everything okay? I heard a noise after you went upstairs." Kyle's eyes travelled to Logan's crotch and back up again.

Oh, god. He can see it. Logan chuckled and tried to disguise his embarrassment. "I tripped going into the bathroom. But I'm fine. Shall we go?"

Although Kyle's SUV was in much better shape than Logan's pick-up truck, they decided to ride in the truck as Logan knew the roads better. As they stepped into the Ford, Logan wrinkled his nose immediately. It smelled like wet dog fur.

"It stinks in here," he said, opening his window. "I was in the lake this afternoon and Buddy was having a good time swimming around. I should've waited for his fur to dry," he said, apologetically.

Kyle chuckled. "That's okay. I don't mind going into the bar smelling like wet dog. Unless it's a fancy bar. Is it?"

Logan now chuckled. "No, no fancy bars tonight. That's reserved for a third date," he said as a joke but felt his cheeks blushing anyway. Kyle also seemed embarrassed. "I'm sorry. I was trying to make a joke."

Kyle smiled. "I knew you were."

Logan smiled back and started the truck. They drove towards Greenville with Logan thankful for the dark woods around his house, hoping they would help disguise his embarrassment. He really couldn't figure out what was wrong with him. His feelings were all over the place. He might as well have been a gangly teenager trying to work them out. He'd never felt this way before and it didn't make any sense to start now. He knew nothing about Kyle apart from the fact he was a cute graphic designer with a kid, and who was getting divorced from his wife. For all Logan knew, he could be a terrible person, and he'd long ago decided he was done with that kind.

They arrived fifteen minutes later at a small bar Logan went to from time to time. Jackie, the owner, was a fifty-year old lady who everyone loved and who Logan suspected was a lesbian. He'd never asked, obviously, but deep down he felt a connection with her, like there was a non-spoken recognition.

They sat at the counter and Logan nodded at Jackie. It was a slow night and the place was pretty much empty besides themselves and a couple of guys playing pool.

Jackie came over to them. "Hey, kiddo. How's everything?"

"Hey, Jackie. Pretty good, actually. I have good news. I got promoted today."

Jackie's grin grew broader. "Aww, really? Congratulations, hon. That's so nice to hear. And you deserve it."

"Thanks."

"So, what are you boys having?"

Logan glanced at Kyle. Jackie had lingered just a smidgen too long on the word 'boys' and Logan felt embarrassed she might think they were an item.

"I'll have a beer."

Kyle asked for one too and Jackie brought them two bottles—on the house.

"You really don't have to," Logan protested.

"It's my pleasure. To help you celebrate your promotion." She winked and left them alone.

Logan was sure she'd offered them complimentary beers because she thought they were on a date together, afraid Kyle might have noticed too. So, instead of looking at him he focused on the TV up above the far side of the counter. It was tuned to some football game he'd no interest in, but he pretended he had as an excuse not to engage in conversation.

"You got promoted?" Kyle asked, putting his beer down and ending a short silence that had seemed like an eternity.

"I did," and Logan at last turned to Kyle, seeing the most beautiful of smiles. "It mainly means I've more work. I'm now solely responsible for the projects I'm working on."

"That's great. Congratulations," Kyle said, lifting his beer in a toast. Logan clinked his bottle against Kyle's and they drank.

"Thanks."

Kyle nursed his beer for a while and then said, "So, does that mean you're the only one responsible for the work you guys are doing for me?"

"Yeah, actually it does. So, when you decide what you want, call me instead of Mr. Shaffer."

Kyle grinned and seemed very happy with himself. "I will."

Logan drank from his beer, feeling awkward. He didn't know how to read Kyle but he was sure something was going on. He kept getting this strange vibe off him that swayed between flirty and polite, and didn't know what to make of it.

"When's your kid visiting?"

Kyle's smile vanished. Logan didn't want to make him uncomfortable, just didn't know how to act around him.

"I don't know yet." Kyle sighed and sipped his beer. "That's one of the reasons I want to clean the house and have a proper bedroom for him. I'm hoping his mother gives up on her threat of never letting me see him again."

"Why would she do that?" Logan was dumbfounded and could not believe someone would do such a thing. Especially to a guy who seemed so sweet. And, truth be told, deep down it struck a chord with Logan, reminding him of his less-than-perfect mother.

Kyle gazed at Logan and held his breath. "It's complicated," he finally ended up saying, turning back to his beer. "But she feels betrayed, and I guess this is her way of coping with it."

Logan scanned Kyle attentively while he drank his own beer. Who would've thought that someone as likeable as him would betray his wife? No wonder she was threatening him with not seeing his son again. Granted, it did seem a bit extreme, but how could he judge when he wasn't in her shoes? He'd never been betrayed by someone he loved, so he could only imagine what it was like.

"Did she catch you in the act?" Logan tried to sound casual about it but was more than eager to know, more than he was willing to admit. That a guy seemingly as cute and pleasant as Kyle was capable of cheating on his wife had pulled the rug from under him.

Kyle frowned at Logan, as though confused. "Caught me in the act? What... Oh, you think I cheated on my wife? Jesus, no!" He seemed genuinely disturbed by the thought and Logan felt like an ass.

"Oh. I'm sorry. I didn't mean to—"

"That's okay. I guess my choice of words could've been better," and Kyle waved his hand in a gesture of truce." He drank the rest of his beer and placed the empty bottle on the counter, then cleared his throat. "Can I tell you something?"

"Sure."

He locked eyes with Logan but seemed hesitant. He opened his mouth to speak but then broke off eye contact and raised his hand to catch Jackie's attention.

"Can I have a gin and tonic, please?"

Jackie nodded and turned to Logan. "Anything for you, hon?"

"Thanks, but I'm good still."

They waited in silence for Jackie to come back with Kyle's drink. Logan suspected he had something big to tell him. Kyle kept rubbing his hands together and stealing peeks at him in a jittery kind of way that was beginning to make Logan nervous too. There were a million-and-one thoughts rushing round his mind right now, including one where Kyle was a murderer or maybe a con artist. When Jackie finally brought the drink, he took a gulp like he'd been walking through the desert and his glass was filled with cool, fresh water. Then he turned to Logan and opened his mouth once more, but then froze, clearly holding his breath for a moment before exhaling sharply.

"I can't blame Jessica for not wanting me to see Ryan. I lied to her. But the truth is I've been lying to myself for so many years now it was like second nature. I didn't think about it, you know? At least, not consciously."

Logan frowned, trying to make sense of Kyle's words, nursing his drink, his eyes locked on the counter.

"This whole mess would've been avoided if I lived my life differently," Kyle continued. "If I hadn't spent so many years trying to impress other people and trying to do what I thought they wanted me to." Kyle stopped himself again but this time only sipped from his drink. Logan remained utterly confused. Had the man been impersonating someone in the past few years? Maybe he was from a poor family and had tried to pass himself off as some rich kid? But then, Logan's mind was also now serving him up much grimmer scenarios, a hired assassin being one.

Kyle sighed raggedly and drank once more from his gin and tonic. Then he seemed to gather his strength before resolutely turning to face Logan. "I'm gay."

Chapter Nine

Confessing to Logan he was gay was one of the toughest things Kyle had ever done. But now he felt relieved, like someone had instantly lifted a massive weight from his shoulders. Besides Jessica, Logan was the first person he'd told and he was afraid of how he might react. Kyle had spent the entire day thinking of him. How Logan's sturdy frame made him sweat. How his ass was one of the finest he'd ever seen. How his smile made his knees weak. All those feelings had bombarded him relentlessly throughout the day, keeping him from concentrating on his work. It was as if everything he'd suffocated in his teens and early twenties was now bubbling up to the surface at the same time, like a steamy pressure built up over years upon years of heavy denial. He didn't know how else to explain it or the power that was overwhelming him.

So, during the day, as he'd done so many times before, Kyle had tried to ignore his feelings and decided to get on with his house chores, although he continued to feel compelled to talk with Logan and be near him. He scrubbed the kitchen while listening to music, trying to block every thought out of his mind. Then he went to the bathroom and did the same. At three in the afternoon he'd decided he'd cleaned enough for one day and booted up his laptop. He was running behind on Eric's project and had postponed it enough. Between what was happening with Jessica and now Logan, it had been really hard to concentrate for the past few weeks. But he had to suck it up and focus, or he could end up losing this project and the money he was counting on.

After almost three hours of procrastinating, intertwined with brainstorming, he gave up. He'd gone far enough for this day and couldn't squeeze another idea out of his mushy brain. He decided to take a shower and drop by Shaffer & Hamilton Woodworks. He wanted to see Logan. With what excuse he didn't know, but he'd come up with something. He'd say he was interested in some piece of furniture he'd seen in the catalogue Logan had given him, but had some questions about the wood or something. And as he couldn't focus on anything else, he might as well give in to temptation. Maybe that way he'd flush Logan out of his brain once and for all.

Logan wasn't at the workshop, hadn't been all afternoon, and now Kyle didn't know what else to do. He almost asked Logan's boss for his home address but didn't at the last moment. It'd be too weird and hugely inappropriate. He ended up driving back home, indecision having made his mind freeze. His teenage-like feelings kept boiling up inside him, though, mixed with the guilt of feeling like he was failing his son. But he'd been over this before. There was no shame in wanting to be happy and a better person. Ryan could only benefit from having a well-balanced father. And lately, Kyle had felt like he was reaching a tipping point. There was a mix of emotions swirling inside him, pressurizing his skin from underneath, making it hard to breath and deal with everyday life. He had to do something about it or he would crack under the tidal forces that threatened to rip him apart.

Kyle now remembered Logan saying his house was nearby, so he decided he'd drive around until he found it. It was almost twilight but he couldn't stay home and do nothing at all. He'd find Logan's house and invite him to have a beer, just like they had talked about that morning.

He spent a good hour driving around, glancing at the map on his phone and trying not to get lost, but finally managed to find Logan. It was almost night time and he'd been about to give up, but when he spotted his truck, Kyle's mouth almost fell open. Logan emerged from his garage bare-chested, like some Greek god shedding his bright light over the mortals around him. As if that wasn't enough, Kyle was knocked out by Logan's pure demeanor. It was as if he hadn't a clue about the effect he had on other people.

Logan seemed surprised to see him and, Kyle would say, even slightly embarrassed. Deep down, the teenager in him wished it was because Logan was also gay and had feelings for him. Kyle had spent his entire life hearing about how gay people had a "Gaydar", a finely-tuned means of detecting other gays. But his was mute. Maybe he didn't have one. Or maybe he needed to give it time to start working. Nevertheless, there was something about the way Logan looked at him that made him think that maybe, just maybe, he could also be gay. He feared this was all wishful thinking, of course. He hadn't the first clue about what to expect of gay men beyond the stereotypes he'd been exposed to all his life. This also made him insecure because he didn't know how to behave or what to expect. He had so many questions. Unfortunately, he didn't have anyone he could ask them of, and, he suspected, porn wasn't the answer.

The trip with Logan to Greenville had fortunately been under the blanket of night, giving Kyle the opportunity to compose himself. He'd seen the contour of Logan's penis pressed against his jeans when he'd come into the living room fresh from the shower, and tried his best to be as indifferent to it as possible. He didn't really know if it had worked or not but knew his face felt warm and he probably looked flushed.

Logan had taken him to a cozy bar with a lovely lady working behind the counter. Kyle felt the pressure inside his chest building up and wanted to confide in him, to tell him everything and hope for the best. There was something about Logan that made him feel like he could talk to him, and he didn't expect anything from him other than a friendly ear. Maybe then that hurricane of emotions would simmer down and let him breath again. And then Logan had gone and thought he'd cheated on Jessica because of his poorly chosen words… He didn't want Logan thinking he was capable of cheating on anyone. That had been exactly why he'd stayed for so long with Jessica without ever acting on his feelings. No, he had to tell Logan what was going on. He had to tell him.

The whirlwind inside him spun faster as their conversation progressed, and when the wave of emotions threatened to drown him, Kyle simply said, "I'm gay."

***

Logan blinked at Kyle's confession and tried not to grin. His heart beat furiously in his ears. He didn't know what to say. There was a sense of glee growing inside him for which he immediately felt guilty, knowing that being gay was the cause of Kyle's divorce and his wife threatening to forbid him from ever seeing his son again. The poor guy. Logan wanted to hold him in his arms and tell him everything was going to be okay.

"Right," he said instead. The words he really wanted to say insisted on staying glued to the back of his mouth and so a moment of silence ensued. Kyle took another drink of his gin and seemed sadder by the moment. He probably thought Logan was now shunning him. "You don't have to be sad about it, you know."

"Yeah? Well, I don't know what to do. My wife thinks I'm a pervert and says she's never letting me see Ryan again. I practically ran away from all my friends because they're not really my friends, and because I thought I could start a new life away from it all. But now I'm here? I just feel lonely and afraid I'll never see my son ever again, and all down to my own selfishness."

"You're overthinking it."

"How would you know?"

Logan drank from his beer and turned to Kyle. "I've been where you are when I was about sixteen and eventually got over it. And despite what your wife thinks, no judge would agree to keep a father away from his son just because he's not straight."

Kyle pursed his lips. Then he broke off eye contact and drank the rest of his gin and tonic in one go. He turned to Logan again. "You're gay?"

Logan nodded.

"I have so many questions!"

Logan's forehead wrinkled in confusion. He'd assumed Kyle was opening up to him because he was alone in a strange town, but this was now starting to look like he was coming out for the very first time.

"Have you spoken to anyone else about this?"

"Beyond my wife? No, not really."

Logan drank from his beer and took a long, hard look at Kyle. He was pale and a bit sweaty. He seemed nervous, but his sickly look could also be from this damn heat. But no, that wasn't it. The bar was cool enough. His could only be the face of someone who was probably panicking about coming out. Logan quietly sighed.

"I know that right now you're probably freaking out about this, but you really don't have to. You're not alone, and to be honest, I'm pretty surprised you felt like you had to hide it for so long," but then Logan paused. "No, that came out all wrong. What I mean is there is no shame in being who you are. You deserve to be happy, and you shouldn't try to be someone you're not just to please someone else."

Kyle was fiddling with his fingers, his eyes focused on them like they were the most important thing in the world right now. "I really loved her, you know? Or I thought I did. But I couldn't bear it any longer. I was having nightmares on an almost daily basis and there were days when I couldn't breathe. Not even sweating myself into oblivion in the gym made it go away. I was always angry for no reason and we began to fight. I didn't want that for Ryan. I want to be a good father."

Logan's heart ached. "Don't beat yourself up. That won't help you in any way, trust me. And you don't have to explain yourself, not to me and not to anyone else. You don't have to endure a nervous collapse before you're allowed to be happy."

Kyle looked up from the counter at Logan, coming out of his hunched posture. Logan realized how small he'd seemed since they'd got here, considering how tall the guy was, almost taller than him, but that presence was showing again.

"Thank you." A timid smile blossomed on his lips.

Logan didn't think about it, but leaned forward and hugged Kyle, a tight embrace through which Logan tried to show him there was no shame in being who he was. Kyle went as stiff as a log, his arms tight to his sides. But after a moment, he seemed to relax and hugged Logan back. Kyle's large hands landed on Logan's back, their warmth scalding him like a pair of white-hot branding irons. He noticed Kyle smelled of coconut, the same sweet scent he'd smelled when he'd first seen him in the shop, and was overwhelmed by a need to bury his face in his neck. But he couldn't. Kyle was a client and he couldn't mess things up.

Logan leaned back again, Kyle's hands sliding past his ribs. His penis twitched and he avoided looking Kyle in the eye. Instead, he drank the rest of his beer, trying to quench a thirst no beer would ever be able to satisfy. "Want another?" he said, nodding at Kyle's glass.

"Yes, please."

Chapter Ten

They left the bar that night with Logan promising Kyle he wouldn't be alone in Greenville from now on. Logan would help him with this next phase of his life. The hardest part, the first step where Kyle had to be truthful to himself, was already done. Now was just a matter of living each day trying to be who he was instead of how he thought people saw him. Kyle seemed optimistic but a bit sad at the same time, so Logan proposed they went fishing that next weekend.

"It seems like a great idea but I don't really know anything about fishing. I also don't have any equipment," Kyle said.

Logan didn't have any experience in fishing, either. In fact, he'd just bought the fishing rods and had yet to use them.

"I don't know how to fish, either, but it looks relaxing. The lake's beautiful. We can have a couple of beers… I can lend you a fishing rod. As for equipment, how about shorts, T-shirt and a pair of flip-flops? Like you, I don't have any 'proper' equipment. Oh, and bring a cap. The sun's hot around here."

"So, your idea is to sit by the lake drinking beers? Seems fine by me," Kyle said, a wide grin on his face.

***

That Saturday, Kyle drove to Logan's house and they went in Logan's Ford to the lake, as he knew the roads better. Buddy went along, too. It was a beautiful, warm, sunny day. The placid waters were crystal clear by the shore and seemed perfect for a day spent angling. They both wore just T-shirts and shorts as neither had the equipment to spend long hours knee-deep in the water. But it was warm enough, so they could endure some time in it without being too uncomfortable. Or so they thought.

After just one hour of standing more or less still their backs were aching and their skin wrinkly. Buddy didn't help either, as he constantly jumped in and out of the lake, barking and running around, as excited as if it was his first time outside the house. They finally gave up on catching anything because no fish would have come near them in all that commotion. Since their clothes were already wet, Kyle decided to go for a swim. The place was too beautiful not to enjoy it, and that way the trip wouldn't turn out to be a total waste. Logan wasn't in the mood and so stayed on the shore, enjoying a beer, playing with Buddy and pretending he wasn't extremely aware of a semi-naked Kyle now swimming in nothing more than his boxer shorts. Neither of them had thought of bringing swim gear, not in the excitement of planning their trip, and Kyle argued that boxer shorts were practically the same.

Logan almost choked on his beer when Kyle came out of the water, though, his body glistening and his boxers semi-transparent and glued to him. Kyle's penis was pushing against the fabric, its curved shape perfectly visible. Logan swallowed hard and looked away as Kyle lifted the fabric from his skin and twisted it, squeezing excess water out. Logan tried to focus on Buddy and ignore his own tenting shorts, feeling embarrassed and aroused all at the same time. Seeing Kyle like that awakened the same thirst he'd felt in the bar, but it wasn't right for him to do anything about it right now. Kyle was worried about the possibility of losing his son, so Logan reckoned the last thing he'd want on top of that was to have to deal with a horny guy he barely knew.

"You should go for a swim. The water's great," Kyle said.

"Maybe after finishing this one," Logan said, raising his beer.

Kyle shook his head, sprinkling water everywhere, and sat on the grass, observing the place. "Thank you for being there for me," he said after a while, breaking the silence.

"You don't have to thank me. It's the least I could do. It's not easy being truthful to yourself."

Kyle turned to Logan. "Was it easy for you, when you came out?"

Logan's stomach flinched. He didn't want to start answering questions about his youth. "Normal, I guess."

"Did your friends accept you?"

Logan scoffed. Friends… Back then he didn't have any friends. There weren't many kids in the street he grew up in, and the few who lived there were more bullies than anything else. Then again, Logan hadn't been a delicate flower himself while growing up. He couldn't be. The guys who prowled his neighborhood would have smelled his fear, his weakness, and would have preyed on him. He still remembered one day when he was arriving home and saw a kid that lived nearby being beaten to a pulp. He later found out the kid had gone to the police to file a complaint against one of the older guys. With no proof, though, there'd been nothing the police could do. The beating was a reminder, so he knew who was in charge and what happened to snitches who didn't know their place.

It wasn't just the streets that made Logan realize he couldn't afford to be too sensitive. Having a drunken mother who operated an incessant revolving door of lovers, many of them aggressive, made him toughen up real quick. He still recalled the moment he stopped trusting her. It had all begun with a punch that had sent him flying across the bedroom after he'd walked in on Henry, one of his mother's boyfriends, as he was stealing from her. That had been his way of making Logan keep his mouth shut, and his mother believed Henry's story that he'd been teaching Logan a lesson about respect for elders and not talking back. That had been the moment when he finally realized he couldn't count on her. He had been twelve at the time.

"I didn't exactly come out to my friends. I didn't have many. I'd just begun hitting the bars, and one day I realized I wasn't that interested in women." Logan tried not to sound sad about it, but the story made him feel sorry for his former self, the lone teenager trying to figure out things all by himself, ending up doing stupid stuff in the process. He turned to Kyle, who was observing him attentively.

"I'm sorry," Kyle said. "Looks like it must've been really hard for you."

Logan shrugged. "It is what it is."

Kyle stood up and started drying himself on his towel. Logan looked away, pretending to take in the view of the lake, but it was hard to ignore Kyle's sculpted body when it was so close to him. He drank from his beer and petted Buddy who was resting by his side, tongue hanging out of his mouth as he tried to cool down.

"How about your parents? Did you tell them, as well?"

Logan finished his beer and got up, intending to put the empty can in a bag he'd brought for recyclables. He didn't know how to answer Kyle without lying to him. He didn't want to, but he also didn't feel comfortable sharing his whole story with him, not just yet. He raised his eyes from the bag and his train of thought went missing somewhere between getting upright and watching Kyle turn around and drop his boxer shorts to the ground before hopping out of them, his perky ass then staring right at him. Kyle probably hadn't thought much of it, but Logan could by now only listen to the drumming of his heart. His penis twitched harder and he thought of grabbing Kyle by his waist and fucking him right here.

"Oh, my God! Jacob! Jacob, cover Aiden's eyes! Oh my heavenly God!"

The woman's screams startled them both, and Kyle covered his crotch with his towel and turned around at the same time as Logan. Their eyes briefly met and Logan thought he saw something in them, but the earsplitting female screech knocked this and everything else from his mind.

Behind them, twenty yards away, were a middle-aged couple with a small boy and a picnic basket. They had come down the same path Logan and Kyle had used to get there, but then Logan recognized the woman as the one who'd asked him to sign her petition. A rotund man behind her was trying to keep the five- or six-year-old boy from sneaking a peek around him. Logan watched as the woman strode towards them, a thunderous scowl on her face.

"What's the meaning of this?" she demanded as she drew near, her glare of indignation clearly intended to condemn them to Hell.

Buddy was by now barking at the woman and she recoiled, a look of fear flushing her face. Logan grabbed him by his collar. "Easy boy," he said, then turned to the woman. "Stop shouting! You're scaring my dog."

"I'm not shouting!" she said, in an even louder voice.

Buddy was still barking at her. Logan feared he'd jump at the hag and bite her, so he grabbed his collar even tighter. "Buddy here seems to disagree and my ears are sure ringing, so I'd say you're screaming. Could you lower your voice?"

"This country is damned to Hell! A person can't go outside without having to endure a couple of sodomites flaunting their sinful behavior," she almost spat at him.

"What's a 'Somomite', grandpa?" Logan heard the kid ask.

"They're sinners, Aiden, working against God's plan," the man told him.

Logan bit his tongue. "Maybe you should leave, ma'am. I really don't want to drag your grandson into an argument. It's not right."

"Leave?" she snarled. "I'm not going anywhere. You two sinners are the ones who should leave. Look at that one, all naked," she said, pointing at Kyle, as if his nakedness only reinforced what the man had said about them being sinners. "I came here to have a picnic with my grandson and I'm having one. Now, get out of here before I call the police!"

Logan glanced back. Kyle seemed to have shrunk at the hag's jab, which sparked a jolt of adrenaline in Logan's gut that fueled a wave of anger. Something had snapped and he had had enough. He faced down the woman, leaning menacingly over her, and her hand shot to her chest. Her now wide eyes scanned him keenly, as if scared he was going to hurt her.

"You're gonna shut that pie hole of yours and leave because you're being loud and obnoxious, and you're scaring my dog. You're a terrible example to your grandson and you should be ashamed of yourself. If you want to call the cops, then by all means, go right ahead. We're not breaking any laws and maybe they'd like to hear how you spill your hate-speech around a young child."

The woman opened her mouth before spitting, "Are you threatening me?"

"Threatening?" Logan laughed. "Lady, I'm just telling you what you're options are. Now, go somewhere else and leaves us alone. Unless you secretly just want to see my friend, here, naked. Is that it? I think maybe it is."

Her face went from red to white and then to purple. She opened and closed her mouth several times, like a goldfish, seeming to have lost her voice. Turning around, she barked at the man to follow her and together they marched off, the poor kid dragged along at their heels as he complained that he wanted a dog like the "somomites" had.

Logan and Kyle watched them leave in silence. Once they were out of sight, Logan realized how hard he was breathing. His heart was galloping and his hands were cold and clammy. He couldn't remember the last time he'd been in a situation like this. He vaguely recalled once being bullied for liking men and solving the problem by punching the other guy, then leaving for a drink like nothing had happened. But that had been a lifetime ago, when he didn't really care what other people said or how he acted. It was different now, but having the woman screaming insults at him in front of Kyle had left him shaken. It reminded him of those early days and, for a moment, made him fear for how people around here would react when they found out about his past.

Logan turned to Kyle. He was gripping his towel in front of him so hard his knuckles were white.

"What's her problem?" Logan tried to smile but it was plain the verbal skirmish had left Kyle shaken, too.

"I think she really doesn't like the idea we could be together," Kyle said.

Logan took a deep breath. "I'm sorry you had to go through that. People around here aren't normally like that. Consider it your baptism of fire. After this, you're ready to take on the world," and he chuckled, trying to lighten the mood.

"It's all right. I'm not gonna crawl back to the closet, if that's what you're thinking."

"I wasn't." It was exactly what Logan had been thinking.

"Maybe she wouldn't have screamed at us if I hadn't been butt naked. I'm sorry for that. I wasn't thinking. I just wanted to change into my shorts because my underwear was too wet."

"Don't worry about those lunatics. They're crazy."

Kyle scoffed. "I guess the only thing that worries me is the poor kid growing up in that environment, under those values. It could mess up his mind."

Logan knew Kyle was thinking of his son and his heart tightened. "How about we try this again some other day and go for some ice cream? What do you say?"

"I think it's a great idea."

Logan took another deep breath and felt relieved. However unpleasant this episode had been, Logan thought, at least it had distracted Kyle from delving into his past.

Chapter Eleven

"Does it hurt when…" but Kyle stopped himself. He was leaning against the front wall of his house, nursing his coffee as he watched Logan sawing what would be part of his repaired porch. He'd finally decided on the furniture he wanted for Ryan's bedroom and also that he needed to fix his porch. Part of the floor was rotten and he didn't want Jessica screaming at him that he couldn't have his son over on account of a couple of problematic boards.

Logan stopped and straightened. A couple of sweat beads ran down his temples. His T-Shirt was glued to his chest which made Kyle so much more aware of his muscular frame.

"Does what hurt? Sawing? My back's not happy about it, but it doesn't hurt," he said, smiling.

Kyle and Logan had been spending time together since the lake incident, as they were now calling it, and Kyle was loving it. They went out for a beer or a movie, or whatever they'd feel like doing, and he couldn't have been happier about it. Logan was lovely to have around and he really helped him feel a bit more comfortable in his skin. Kyle was now even able to say the word "gay" out loud without cringing, something he'd never been able to do before. The only thing missing, though, was Logan's backstory. He was awfully reserved and avoided talking about his past whenever Kyle brought it up. Kyle didn't want to push him to talk about something he didn't want to, so had decided to wait until Logan was ready. There was probably something in there that still pained him. In Kyle's mind, that something was a couple of abusing parents who had kicked Logan out after discovering he was gay. During that week they had talked a lot about everything, but Kyle still had no clue about how gay sex worked or how he should behave with men, so he thought he could start off by asking Logan for the harmless stuff, like dating advice, before proceeding to what was really bugging him.

Sex.

But now that enough time had gone by to ask the hard questions, Kyle found himself embarrassed. Maybe he should just go online and see what kind of advice the Internet had to offer. He didn't want to, though. He wanted to ask Logan, the man who was on his mind all of his waking hours. His crush had grown and now the only part of the day when he wasn't thinking of Logan was when he was focusing on his several deadlines—and even then it was proving to be a challenge. Kyle had come to realize that Logan was not only handsome but also a sweet guy who went out of his way to help everyone around him, especially his neighbor Mrs. Cook. She was a cute old lady who he now knew was tougher than he'd thought, after seeing her hunched over her garden for the first time.

They'd been returning from town one day and Logan had asked if Kyle would mind driving by, just to check on her before going home. She was delighted to meet Kyle and had looked at him in a weird kind of way that he'd brushed off as curiosity. She then invited them to have dinner, apologizing immediately after realizing she was almost out of olive oil and couldn't season her salad. Without thinking twice, Logan offered to return to town and buy it for her. It had been in that moment that Kyle thought how lucky he was to have met someone like him, so kind and altruistic.

Kyle was now torn between letting it show how much he liked Logan and playing uninterested. Part of it was because he didn't know how to behave, but above all he feared Logan didn't feel the same. And it was easier just to indulge in a fantasy than face a reality where Logan would say he wasn't.

"I wasn't talking about sawing," Kyle said. "It's ..." He sighed. "Never mind."

Logan frowned. "What?"

"Never mind."

Logan placed his hand saw on the improvised sawing table they'd set up on the porch and gazed at Kyle, a hint of a smile twisting his lips. "Come on, you can tell me."

Kyle kept nursing his coffee, the words he wanted to say trapped in a limbo somewhere between his brain and his mouth. It was almost as if every time he wanted to utter them his tongue went limp.

"It's embarrassing. Never mind."

By now, Logan had his hands propped on his hips. "More than being screamed at by that hag?"

Kyle chuckled. "I'd say more than that time when I was trying to take the stone out of that avocado and it ended up flying straight into your forehead."

Logan rubbed where it had hit, just above his eyebrow, as if reminded of the pain. "Damn. It must be something really embarrassing, then. But you can tell me. What are friends for?"

Kyle's gut churned. Friends. That wasn't exactly what he wanted to hear. Maybe he should just suck it up and be grateful he wasn't alone in this. At least he'd gotten a friend out of it, and Logan was proving to be a great one.

"Well, it's about…sex."

"What about it?"

"I've just been wondering how it works between guys… I don't know if I'm comfortable with some of the…stuff."

Logan chuckled. "Will you just tell me what's on your mind? We're not six anymore. You don't have to be ashamed talking about sex."

The word lingered in the air for a moment. Kyle's eyes were locked with Logan's and his penis had tingled at the mention of the word "sex".

"Does butt sex hurt? I meant anal. Anal!" Kyle was trying to muster up the courage to say it coherently but instead found himself just blurting out the words, as if his mouth was suddenly cut loose from his brain.

Logan blushed for a moment before breaking into laughter that made him bend over. He laughed so hard that when he got up there were tears in his eyes. Kyle felt ashamed and slightly angry at his reaction. Why was he making fun of him? It was a perfectly legitimate question.

"Are you making fun of me?"

"Oh, God, no," Logan tried to say as his laughter subsided and he cleaned away his tears. "I'm so sorry. I'm not making fun of you. It was just the way you said it. It was funny. Sweet, but funny."

Kyle squinted and exhaled loudly. He felt mocked. "Forget it."

"No, no, please." Logan approached him. "Look, I'm sorry, I really am. I promise I'm not making fun of you." Kyle hummed a "mm-hmm" while sipping at his coffee and Logan added, "Answering your question: yes, it can hurt a bit, but it's something you only have to do if you want to."

Kyle looked at Logan. He seemed genuinely sorry for bursting into laughter but it didn't matter anymore. Kyle's mind was now focused on his answer. He'd always suspected anal sex would hurt like hell. The only time he'd tried to finger himself he hadn't been able to carry through with it. So the question was why did men do it?

"I've always thought gay sex was mainly that."

Logan smiled. "I think this is going to be a very long talk. Shall we go in? I need something to drink."

In the kitchen, they each sat on a stool around the island. Kyle drank from his coffee but Logan downed in on the glass of water he'd drawn from the tap. Kyle felt uncomfortable about bringing up the subject, but he'd always wondered about it. With women he knew what he technically had to do, and anatomically it wasn't that hard to figure out what went where. But with men? That was a whole different story.

"Welcome to gay sex one-on-one. Full disclaimer here: I don't claim to be an expert," Logan said, smiling at Kyle.

Kyle laughed. "Is that so? Maybe I should go searching for my answers online, with someone who is, then."

"Please be quiet," Logan said in a very teacher-like way. "Let's begin. Your first lesson about gay sex is that you can do whatever the hell you want to, provided you and your partner feel comfortable with it. There are no requirements. You don't have to like anal sex just because you think that's what two guys do. There are lots of people who get off just on frottage, and there's masturbation, blow jobs—"

"What's frottage?"

"It's when you and your partner rub on each other's bodies. A fancy word I've learned when I was in j—" Logan seemed suddenly distressed about something, but before Kyle could ask him what was wrong, he went on: "A word I learned a while ago. There are lots of things you can do that can be considered sex without penetration."

Kyle was so fascinated he quickly forgot about Logan's apparent distress. "I had never thought of that. It seems so obvious now, but before you said it out loud, I thought 'sex' was when... Well, you know."

"I know what you mean, but don't stress about it. Sex is whatever you want it to be, as long as you feel comfortable with it."

Kyle sipped on his coffee once more. That cleared things up a lot, but he was still wondering. "But if it hurts, why do people do it?"

"You mean anal sex?"

"Yeah."

Logan smiled. "For one thing it doesn't hurt. And it's damn good, especially if you're connected with that special someone and you can relax enough to enjoy it."

"It is?"

"Yup. It's awesome for several reasons, but mainly because it stimulates your prostate. If you haven't had a prostate-induced orgasm, you don't know what you're missing."

Kyle felt himself blush. All this talk about sex was getting uncomfortable, and not because he felt embarrassed. He wasn't a virgin anymore, but the more Logan explained stuff, the more Kyle wanted to do…things to him.

"Well, thanks for explaining how this stuff works but I have to return to my work. I still have a bunch to do and my deadline's this Friday."

Logan tilted his head. "Are you okay?"

"Yeah. Why do you ask?"

"You seem uncomfortable. Is it because I laughed? I promise I wasn't making fun of you."

Kyle suppressed a smile. It was endearing, really, to see Logan so worried about him. "I know. Don't worry about that. I'm just not that comfortable yet. I know this is all perfectly fine and normal but it's difficult to change the way you face a subject after so many years in denial."

"It gets easier, okay? And if you ever want to talk about this again, I want you to know that I'm here for you." Logan's smile warmed Kyle's heart. "Well, I better return to work, too." Logan stood up and placed his glass on the counter then nodded and left the kitchen.

Kyle went into his office and opened his laptop. Logan was becoming a good friend and he was grateful for that. But, at the same time, his attraction for him wasn't subsiding and Kyle didn't know which part he preferred Logan to play: friend or lover. His horny, teenager-self screamed "Lover" every time he thought this, but his more rational side, the adult in him, wanted Logan to be his friend. Kyle needed someone on whom he could lean and rely when he needed to open up. And it was so much easier to confide in someone who knew the real him from the start. Kyle still didn't feel comfortable having "The talk" with his friends, the one where he'd have to tell them he liked men after all and hadn't been entirely truthful with them.

As he was about to focus on his work, his phone chimed with a reminder about Ryan's pediatrician appointment. It was only a routine visit but his heart ached and he felt like the worst father in the history of mankind for not being there. The reminder made him forget about Logan and his crush. That was meaningless without Ryan. He missed him so much. What if Jessica went through with her threat? How would he carry on with his life?

Kyle put his phone down and doubled down on work. He would finish it that night and drive to Jessica's apartment to see his son. He didn't care what she might say. She couldn't prevent him from seeing his own son.

Chapter Twelve

It had been another tiresome day at Shaffer & Hamilton Woodworks. Kyle had left Greenville four days before to visit his son and try to mend his strained relationship with Jessica, and Logan had dived head first into his work, tirelessly sawing, shaving and sanding, trying to pretend he didn't miss him. In the past weeks, Logan had grown to like Kyle and his complexities. Kyle was a six-foot-one, broad-chested man who, beneath his solid frame, hid a sweet guy trying to become a better person and a better parent. He was nothing like the men Logan had known before coming here, as muscular and sensitive didn't normally go hand in hand. And it was endearing to find out that someone that big had so many questions about sex. It made him more human, in a way. Now, though, Logan just had to constrain that bubbly feeling that sprang into life inside his chest every time he thought of him.

He had spent the last four days thinking of the reasons why he shouldn't ask Kyle out on a date. He kept going back and forth over it, but always returned to him being a client he couldn't afford to lose. He couldn't risk it, and he didn't want to put Kyle in an awkward position of having to reject his advances. Especially now, not so soon after he'd come out. Even if he asked him for a date and Kyle said yes, did he want the responsibility of being the first man he'd ever gone with? He didn't feel up to the task. Certainly there were better guys out there, ones more suited to Kyle—guys who hadn't been in jail. He'd begun to think he could tell him about his past but had yet to muster up the courage. He couldn't bring himself to be honest with him, for deep down he feared he'd lose him over it. Who in his right mind would want to date an ex-felon?

Logan headed home, his mind wrapped up in uncertainty about how to proceed with Kyle. The late afternoon sun was still hot in the sky and Logan felt roasted and sticky inside the Ford. He drove leisurely, windows cranked open, the sweet-scented breeze flowing through, carrying with it the aromas of pine and fern. As usual, he drove by Mrs. Cook's house. She waved and he turned into her driveway. As he pulled in, Logan thought how his neighbor was one of the most active people he knew. She seemed to live outside, always tending to her garden and vegetables.

"Hi, Mrs. Cook. Everything okay?" he said, jumping out of his pickup truck.

"Everything's fine, dear. I'm glad I saw you. I have something for you," she said, her hair bun wiggling as she nodded.

Logan kissed her on her cheek. "You do?"

"Come." She went inside and Logan followed. In the kitchen, Mrs. Cook had a bag of dog snacks and a bunch of great smelling herbs on her counter. She picked them up and turned to Logan, saying, "I was in town today and these cookies reminded me of Buddy. They're supposedly great at preventing gum disease, so I bought them for him. And this is oregano from my garden I've had drying up for the past couple of weeks. I know how you love your salads, and this is so much tastier than that stale stuff they sell at the store."

Logan's nose was assaulted by the wonderfully strong scent of the dried oregano and he couldn't help but smile. "Thank you, Mrs. Cook. What would I do without you?" and he took the dog biscuits and the herbs.

"My pleasure, dear."

"I better get going. Buddy will be hungry by now. I forgot to top up his bowl this morning."

"Oh, that reminds me. I think you have a visitor." Mrs. Cook smile was a mixture of giddiness and a touch of teasing.

"I do?"

"Yes. I saw your friend driving by an hour ago and his car hasn't returned since."

Logan's heart jumped. Kyle was back?

"You mean Kyle?" She nodded. "Okay. Thanks again for these, Mrs. Cook," he said, admiring the gifts in his hands.

"Don't mention it. Now, scram. That friend of yours must be hungry, too." She winked and Logan smiled as he left, feeling a bit embarrassed. He wasn't entirely sure why Mrs. Cook had winked, but there was something in the way she acted when Kyle was around that made Logan feel as if she thought they were a couple.

Logan started the Ford and drove off, trying not to push the gas pedal too much. He was feeling too excited about having Kyle back and needed to take it down a notch. He wondered why he hadn't called, to tell him he was coming back, but he'd find out soon enough.

A couple of minutes later, he pulled in next to Kyle's SUV. He was inside, his seat leaned back and the windows open, a bored expression on his face. He straightened at the sound of Logan's Ford and broke into a smile. Logan turned off the engine and jumped out, smiling back at him.

"Why didn't you call to say you were arriving today? I could've fixed us something for dinner," he said, going around his truck and approaching Kyle's SUV. He was already out and waiting for him, his hand stretched out to shake Logan's.

"It was meant to be a surprise but I should've thought of the heat. It's brutal out here."

Logan scanned him and noticed how his fair skin was now reddish and covered in small droplets of sweat. He shook his hand. "You could've gone under those trees. It's cooler there."

"I tried that but then my ass began to hurt, sitting for too long on those roots."

Logan laughed. "Come on in," and he grabbed Mrs. Cook's gifts from his truck. "How was the trip? I want to know everything." He opened the front door and heard Kyle sigh.

"Meh. Could've been worse, I guess. At least I saw Ryan and was able to have an almost civilized conversation with Jessica. She insisted on having a couple of our friends there as witnesses, though."

"Witnesses?" Logan said as they walked into the house. The air inside was refreshing and his body relaxed immediately. Buddy came running up to them, barking as he jumped around them as if it was Christmas. Logan gave him a couple of the cookies Mrs. Cook had bought, to keep him busy, then turned to Kyle. He didn't want Buddy interrupting them. "But why would she want people there? Is she afraid to be alone with you?"

"I don't think so. I'm guessing she wanted someone to use against me in case I said something that could help her get sole custody of Ryan."

Logan looked at Kyle in disbelief. "Really? She'd do that?"

"I don't know. I hope not. I don't think she really meant to use them as witnesses. She probably just wants me to suffer like I've made her suffer."

Logan tried to put himself in Jessica shoes, but still couldn't even start to imagine how big the sense of betrayal would be. "I imagine it's not an easy situation for the both of you," he ended up saying, lost for words.

Kyle smiled. "It's not. But I managed to make some progress. I persuaded Jessica to consider coming over and seeing how the house is still the same, save for the lack of dust and the new floor on the porch. I want to show her I'm not turning it into some kind of freak show, with sex-swings all over the place."

Logan frowned, feeling Kyle's notion of what a freak show was to be somewhat offensive. "You know, it'd be perfectly fine if that was the case. I mean, what gets your rocks off has nothing to do with your character. You can be having nothing but missionary sex with your wife and still be a dickhead."

Kyle blinked a couple of times. "Oh, I'm…I'm sorry. I didn't mean to…to offend you. If that's what you're into, I—"

"What? No! I'm not saying I'm into that kind of stuff," Logan said, watching Kyle's face blush. "I'm just saying you shouldn't be quick to dismiss people based only on their sexual fetishes."

"You're right. I hadn't thought of it that way."

Kyle's neck had almost vanished into his shoulders and his hands were deep into his jeans pockets. If contrite were a person, he'd be it. Logan chuckled.

"I'm just saying things are not black and white. But forget about it. What did she say? Is she coming?"

Kyle shrugged. "I don't know. I really hope so, but she didn't want to promise me one way or another."

"I wish I could help, but I really don't know what to do. The only thing I can offer right now is a tasty homemade dinner. What do you say?"

A smile crept back onto Kyle's lips. "Can't say no to that."

Logan grinned. "Do you like meatballs?"

"Sure."

"Meatballs it is, then."

Talking with Kyle was easy. Before Logan realized it, dinner was ready and served: meatballs and spaghetti with tomato sauce, accompanied by salad seasoned with Mrs. Cook's oregano. They sat at the kitchen table, talking about Kyle's dreams of being a good father and not letting this new chapter in his life ruin the one thing he'd done right: his son. Logan was entranced by the candor of his words, trying to remember the reason he'd promised himself he wouldn't try to kiss him, but it was getting harder by the minute. The way Kyle talked about himself, the way his eyes sparkled every time he mentioned Ryan, made Logan's chest ache. He just wanted to hold him tight and tell him everything would be okay.

The spell was broken when Kyle looked at his watch. "Oh, I've gotta run. I've some final fixes I need to work on before delivering that project."

Logan's heart sank, echoing his disappointment. While he completely understood Kyle's need to go, he was hoping they could have kept talking the whole night through. It was the least Kyle could do after disappearing for four long, never-ending days.

"So soon? Don't you want dessert before you go?" Logan's disappointment must have been all too revealing. He tried to compose himself by smiling, but he was sure it looked lame.

"I want, but I can't. I really have to finish this. But we can do something tomorrow if you want. How about catching a movie or going for ice cream?"

Logan's heart settled right back in place. "Sounds great," he said, already counting the minutes.

Chapter Thirteen

As Logan's house shrank in the SUV's rearview mirror, Kyle hated himself for being such a wuss. But things had become too real for a moment and he'd panicked, not knowing how to act or what to do. The dinner had been going great up until they'd finished their meal and Logan had started gazing at him in a way that made his insides melt and his heart beat faster. There was something in his eyes, something Kyle thought he'd recognized as desire but wasn't sure of. His body had reacted with sweat, dizziness and a slight knot in his stomach, and after ten long minutes of making small talk, he'd decided he couldn't take it anymore. He wasn't lying when he'd said he had work to do, but there was no need to flee Logan's house like that. Idiot! How would he ever be happy if he kept avoiding acting on his feelings? How would he find out if what he felt was real or just a byproduct of everything he'd been ignoring for so long? Was he being selfish if, by trying to navigate his maze-like feelings, he ended up hurting Logan?

Kyle slammed his hand on the steering wheel. It was all too complicated and overwhelming. The only thing he knew for sure was that Logan was constantly on his mind and those thoughts were impossible to push away. These past four days away from Logan had been almost as difficult as when he'd decided to tell Jessica the truth. The only thing that made it tolerable was the sparkle in Ryan's eyes when he'd arrived at Jessica's apartment. Ryan had fled his mother's arms as soon as he saw Kyle crossing the door's threshold, saying "Dada, dada", glee plastered all over his little face. In that moment, everything went away: his doubts, his fears, Logan, everything except for that little fella who put so much trust and love in him.

Kyle pulled up in his driveway. Ryan was one of the big reasons he'd decided to come out in the first place. He wanted to be a better man, a better father, and leave behind the bitter shell of the person into which he had been transforming. What was he so afraid of, anyway? The first step, the hardest one, was now done. From here on in he only had to be honest with Logan and tell him what he really felt.

**

Kyle and Logan were eating ice cream, sitting on the truck's cargo area, feet dangling just above the ground. The scorching sun was too much to bear and they had parked the car under the shade of a tree. Kyle had spent the previous night and that whole day thinking of Logan and how he needed to tell him how he felt. He'd come to the conclusion that there was no way of postponing that conversation any longer. So he'd driven by Logan's work that afternoon to challenge him to go for the ice cream they'd talked about the previous night. Logan hadn't been too sure if he should, given he was in his work clothes and in need of a shower, but ended up accepting the challenge without seeming to give it too much further thought. After buying way too much of the dessert, they'd driven up to the lake to enjoy the cooler air and the wonderful views.

Kyle brought the tiny plastic spoon to his mouth and focused on the coolness of the ice cream. Swiss chocolate delight. He closed his eyes and sighed, trying to muster up the courage he needed to speak to Logan. Instead, he stayed silent, listening to the sounds around him: the birds singing nearby, the trees rustling every time the breeze picked up, the soft music coming from the car radio.

"I'm glad we came out here," Logan said. Kyle opened his eyes and looked at him. He was smiling. "It's a beautiful day and so peaceful. I don't even remember anymore why I thought I needed to shower." Logan turned his smile away from Kyle and ate a bite from his ice cream. His eyes were now focused somewhere beyond the lake.

"You don't remember? Well, you should," Kyle said, pinching his nose.

"Shut up," Logan countered, chuckling as he jabbed his knuckles against Kyle's shoulder.

Kyle's laughter quickly subsided. He lowered his head and stared at some pebble on the ground, so he wouldn't have to focus his attention on Logan. "I've been meaning to tell you something. I… I wanted you to know that I'm really grateful for everything you've done. It means a lot to me."

"Don't worry about it. I'm happy to help."

Logan punched him gently on his shoulder again as the words whirled around Kyle. He looked up. Logan was now gazing at him, seemingly perusing his soul. Kyle wanted to tell Logan what he really meant to him but couldn't bring himself to. Those were powerful words that, once said, would be real and palpable, and then out of his control. He could hear his heartbeat drumming in his ears, the noise drowning out the otherwise peaceful woods. His hands were clammy and cold, and it wasn't because of the ice cream cup they held. Kyle could sense the magnetism exuding from Logan's eyes, drawing him ever closer. It was as if the man had his own gravitational field in which Kyle had been caught. No matter how hard he tried, there was nothing else he could do but fall into him.

Kyle's synapses kept firing away at the speed of light while he tried to say what he'd intended to say in the first place. All the while, he kept slowly approaching Logan without realizing it, his lips ajar while he fell into him. When, in between random thoughts, Kyle noticed what he was about to do, he panicked, his mind showing him images of Logan rejecting his kiss, of him telling him how they could only be friends because he didn't feel the same way. In that second it took his lips to meet Logan's, his fears didn't come to pass and he'd already kissed him. Kyle's brain lit up in a storm of fireworks and he pressed in again to taste Logan, an electric whirlwind traveling through his whole body, making him shiver. It was the most exquisite experience Kyle had ever had. He'd no idea it could be like this. Not even in his dreams had it felt so good.

The kiss lasted but a second. Kyle was already parting his lips from Logan, a mixture of shame and happiness spreading through him. He opened his eyes, eager to see if he was mad or not, trying to find some clue as to what to expect. Logan remained frozen, blushing, his eyes darting all over Kyle's face. Its meaning could have been anything.

"I'm sorry. I don't know what came over me." He stopped himself but then continued: "No. Actually, that's not true. Lately, I've found myself attracted to you. I've been meaning to tell you this for so long. It was actually why I came by your work today and tempted you out here. I'm sorry for putting you in this position. It was selfish of me but I can't stop thinking about you, and I guess I thought that maybe... Well, that maybe you could also like me. I don't know. I'm rambling, but the truth is I don't know how to act around men and...and maybe it's time for me to shut up."

Kyle sighed, but before he could say or think of anything else, Logan leaned in and kissed him, mashing their mouths together, his hands holding Kyle's head in place like he was afraid he would run away. Kyle's senses focused on nothing but what was happening: the kiss, and Logan's sweetness that made him shudder and tingle with a mixture of happiness and desire.

"I've been wanting to do this since I first saw you," Logan said, having drawn away from his lips and leant back. His gaze fell on Kyle like he was seeing him for the first time, as though he was trying to record every detail.

Kyle's chest swelled as a bubbly feeling grew inside him. "Really?" he hardly breathed, then smiled in response to Logan's smile.

"Yes, but you're a customer and I was afraid to mess things up and lose my boss potential business."

"So you think it's weird that we've kissed because you're basically working for me?" Kyle teased.

"Shut up," and Logan punched him again on his shoulder.

"I promise I won't hold it against your boss should you mess things up and end up being a terrible kisser."

Logan chuckled and they both fell silent, gazing at each other.

"What happens now?" Kyle said.

Logan pursed his lips. "We take things slowly and see how it goes. Maybe we should keep this to ourselves for now; just until we're sure of what this is."

Kyle smiled but felt a bit hurt. If Logan wasn't sure of what this was then perhaps they weren't really in tune—or he was just overthinking it. It wasn't just that Kyle didn't know how to act around other men; he'd never been very good at dating to start with. As a teenager, girls had seemed to flock to him naturally without much effort on his part. In his early twenties, he was already engaged to Jessica and certain he'd live the rest of his life with her. And now he felt he was starting over and learning everything from the beginning, a whole new world of rules ahead of him to catch up on. His natural inclination to label things, to label people and situations, told him they should be boyfriends now, since they liked each other and had just kissed. But his mature self looked down on the teenager in him and scoffed, thinking he had to grow up and stop labeling everything. He'd be happier that way. Just let things flow.

"Want to have dinner at my place?"

Logan's question broke the silence and Kyle's train of thought. He breathed in slowly, realizing he'd been stuck overthinking everything that had happened in the past few minutes. Now he sensed how the air brimmed with delicate odors and how the sun shone down through the trees, casting intricate shadow patterns on the ground. Life felt like a wonderful gift that he wanted to savor in its entirety.

"Sounds like a great plan."

Logan smiled and kissed Kyle again, but briefly, before saying, "But first I have to make sure you don't have any doubts about my skills as an amazing kisser."

Chapter Fourteen

The kiss had been unexpected but felt like the best thing that had happened to Logan in a very long time. As they drove to his house, the memory of Kyle's soft, warm lips made him feel happy like he didn't remember ever having felt before. Even before ending up in jail, he didn't recall being truly happy. His life had been a series of quick thrills whose sole purpose had been to make him forget about everything he was miserable about: his impoverished life, his unknown father and absent mother, the crime-ridden neighborhood he'd grown up in. His grandmother used to read him stories about loving families and enchanted princes and princesses, which were probably meant to make him forget about his dreary reality, but instead had made him realize what he was missing out on from a very young age. There had been a lot of anger and foolishness back then. He regretted it. And now he was afraid his younger, idiot self would come back to haunt him and screw up the few good things he now had in his life.

Logan took a peek at Kyle. After so many days battling against himself, uncertain how he should deal with the attraction he felt, it was funny to realize Kyle had taken the first step. Kyle. The guy who was juggling so much at the same time: his insecurities about coming out, accepting he was gay, fighting the feeling of being selfish for trying to be happy instead of focusing exclusively on his son. Even with so much on his plate, Kyle had taken the first step.

From now on, there would be no more excuses. Logan would focus on exploring whatever it was he was feeling for Kyle without worrying about being ready. He would also forget about being the right man for him. He would allow himself to be happy without feeling he didn't deserve it, without listening to that shame that weighed down on his shoulders and told him there were better guys out there for Kyle.

Logan snapped back to reality when Kyle placed his hand on his thigh. He was smiling and Logan just wanted to become lost in his eyes. But he had to focus on the road. Logan slid his hand to Kyle's and held it, squeezing it tightly, feeling the warmth of his touch. Kyle's smile grew and Logan's worries were blown away by the warm contentedness that wafted between them. In that moment, he didn't really care what his brain was worrying about. He just wanted to listen to his heart.

***

The silence of the night was pierced only by the sound of the cicadas around them. Logan and Kyle were outside his house, sitting on the porch swing Logan had just installed while Buddy napped inside. Along with the cicadas' song, the gentle back and forth movement rocked Logan into a drowsy state. Kyle was leaning against him, a mug of hot coffee in his hands. The sky was a velvety dark-blue laden with billions of stars, slightly blurred by Logan's sleepiness. Back when he lived in the city, he'd almost never looked up into the sky. But here, free of tall buildings, of lights and pollution, it was impossible not to, and to wonder at the magnificence of it all. He could even see the Milky Way's trail above him, something he'd never even realized existed before moving to Greenville.

Dinner had been wonderful. Between the tasty food and Kyle's kisses, life had seemed good and finally falling into place. Funny how simple things were more enjoyable when there was a special someone to share them with. The only thing bothering Logan now was the struggle he was having with himself regarding how far to go with Kyle that night. By now, the old Logan would be having sex with him, satisfying that need that pulsed stronger than ever inside him and made his blood thicker. But he wasn't that person anymore and Kyle had never been with a man before. He needed to ignore the fire burning within him and focus on the right thing to do.

"Are you sleeping?" Kyle whispered.

Logan had just shut his eyes, trying to think of nothing. "No," he said, smiling. For the past ten minutes or so he'd been under the impression that Kyle was enjoying the beauty of the night. Now he suspected he'd been watching him, instead.

Kyle bent over the bench and placed his coffee mug on the floor beside it. He leaned over Logan again, staring deeply into his eyes. Logan could feel Kyle's heartbeat against him.

"Thank you for everything," he said.

"What do you mean?"

"You've been here for me since I arrived in Greenville. Honestly, I think I'd still be a mess if it wasn't for you."

Logan's smile expanded into a grin. He wrapped his arms around Kyle and kissed him. After parting lips he said, "You don't need to thank me."

Kyle kept his eyes focused on him for a moment and then leaned in for another kiss. Their lips touched gently at first and Logan tasted that sweetness that seemed a part of him. Kyle's tongue began to explore his mouth and their kiss went from tender to feverish. Kyle almost climbed over Logan, and by now he was very aware not only of Kyle's heartbeat throwing punches through their clothes but also of a volume expanding south of his waist. Adrenaline surged and rushed through Logan's body the moment he realized what was pressing against him, a wave of lust washing over him and making him grab Kyle tighter. His mouth went dry and his hips thrust against Kyle, almost involuntarily. His own cock now throbbed in anticipation, the confines of his pants making his erection painful.

And then…it was over.

Kyle slid back to his side of the bench, panting and disheveled. Logan straightened himself, confused and disappointed, his blood boiling.

"Are you okay?" he asked Kyle, sliding next to him.

Kyle was still panting. His eyes seemed feverish under the dim light that seeped through the windows of the house. "Yeah. I'm sorry. I thought I wanted this but I'm not sure I'm ready."

Logan took in a deep breath, suddenly realizing Kyle was probably terrified and turned on all at the same time by the prospect of having sex with a man. Logan should be the bigger man and make sure things were taken slowly, show him how good it could be if done right. He should've done exactly what he'd told Kyle before, by the lake. Why had he let his dick take over?

"Don't worry. It's my fault. Remember when I said we should take things slowly? It's only natural to be nervous about this. You've spent too many years around women, but I'm going to fix that."

Logan's mischievous smile didn't go unnoticed. Kyle laughed and the tension vanished.

"Thanks. It's not like I'm a virgin, you know?"

"I know. Unless your kid is some kind of a miracle." Logan chuckled and punched Kyle on his shoulder.

Kyle grimaced and opened his mouth in fake disbelief. "Funny. Very funny, mister. Don't worry because in a couple of make out sessions I'll show you exactly why the ladies can't get enough of me."

Logan laughed. "The ladies? The ladies can't get enough of you? Really?"

"What? You don't believe me? I'll have you know my smile is deadly. I swear: if I show my teeth in the wrong place, I find myself swarmed by swooning women."

Logan covered his face with one hand and laughed. Then he looked at Kyle. "Oh my god. Let's make a pact, shall we? You don't act like a Don Juan wannabe and I won't make fun of you."

Kyle laughed. "Okay, okay. I promise."

They locked eyes. Kyle's smile was so pure and irresistible Logan felt a need to protect him from harm's way. This kind, sweet man deserved to be happy and Logan would make him so. It was funny to think that way, given that Kyle was almost as tall and as solid as him.

"What?" Logan said, sensing a question in Kyle's eyes.

"I was just wondering about how you were in your teens."

Logan shrugged. "Normal, I guess. Like everyone else."

"Have you always known you were gay or did you like girls when you were younger?"

"Hmm." Logan frowned. That was a very good question. He didn't ever remember being into girls, or rather, being attracted to them. "I think I was aware I was gay from a very early age. Well, I didn't know I was gay because I didn't think of it that way, but I knew there was something different about me. I guess I only became aware of it in my early teens because all the guys were boasting about what they wanted to do with girls and I was more interested in seeing them naked in the locker room. I never felt attracted to women and I don't think I could get aroused if I tried to have sex with one." Kyle seemed to be processing what Logan had said. "How about you? Are you still attracted to women? I mean, how did that work with your wife?" Kyle's expression changed and Logan thought that maybe he'd gone too far.

"I guess I don't feel particularly attracted to women but I never let myself think I was gay. I never thought of it openly but it was always there, lingering in the back of my mind. For me it was only natural to pursue a relationship with a woman. When I met Jessica, I was young and everything made me horny." Kyle chuckled. "Back then it wasn't too hard to get hard." Kyle's chuckle morphed into a brief laugh that soon died away. "But I didn't really enjoy having sex with Jessica. It was far from good. It was more an automatic, biological affair, you know? It pains me to admit it, and I feel embarrassed, because it's like I was using her to hide my sexuality. But it was never remotely as good as I wished it to be." Kyle shrugged.

"And after Ryan was born I gradually lost all interest in sex. It became harder to pretend I was straight, I suppose."

Logan hugged Kyle, and when he leaned back, he said, "You shouldn't feel ashamed for what you did. You were just trying to understand what you were going through, and although you ended up making Jessica suffer in the process, it's not like it's been a walk in the park for you, either. I'm not saying what you did was right but you didn't do it on purpose. Don't punish yourself too hard, okay? You'll end up being best friends. You'll see. And she's still young. I'm sure she'll find love again—true love."

Kyle sighed. "Maybe you're right but I feel terrible because of it."

Logan hugged Kyle harder, squeezing him like that would make everything right, then he leaned back again. "You know what would make you feel better?"

"What?"

"If we practiced kissing. I bet it would make you feel more comfortable around a man."

"Shut up," Kyle said in between chuckles.

"How about this: we go away for the weekend, just the two of us, and you forget about everything: Jessica, your guilt. What do you say?"

Kyle leaned away from Logan and sat up straight, locking eyes with him. "Are you serious?"

"Deadly serious."

"But we've hardly begun dating."

"Is there some unspoken rule about the amount of time you have to be with someone before traveling together?"

"I don't think so," Kyle stammered.

Logan smiled. "There's your answer, then. Besides, it's not like we met yesterday. I was thinking we could go to a place I know. It's nearby, a couple hours' drive."

Logan's smile soaked into Kyle and wiped the sad demeanor from his face. "Let's do it."

Chapter Fifteen

The supermarket was unusually full. People were busying themselves around the snacks and drinks, and Kyle thought that everyone had had the same idea as Logan: to go away for the weekend. He tried to reach for a large bottle of water without bumping into an old lady who was clearly undecided about which soft drink to choose.

"It's for my grandson. He's coming to visit and I don't know what he likes. It's been ages since the last time my daughter visited," she told him, an unsure expression in her eyes.

Kyle felt sorry for her. "If it were me, I'd buy him something else. Something with no artificial coloring and less sugar, maybe. Those things are terrible for the health of the kids."

"They are?"

After that, Kyle was drawn into explaining that most of the drinks arrayed before her had excessive amounts of sugar. He ended up recommended her something healthier, hoping he himself wouldn't end up like her in a few years, not really knowing what his own son liked. When Kyle finally bade her goodbye, he tried to forget about her and the grandson she hadn't seen for so long. He wasn't the old lady and wouldn't dwell on it. Besides, he'd promised Logan he wouldn't think of Jessica or feel guilty about his son for the whole weekend.

Kyle tried to find Logan in the busy store. They had split tasks twenty minutes earlier, so as to leave town as soon as possible. And although Logan was tall and his head would be easily spotted above the sea of people, Kyle spent a good five minutes wandering around. When he finally saw him, he seemed to be hoarding up on tangerines.

"You're not thinking of feeding on that the whole weekend, are you?" Kyle said.

Logan turned to him. "I'll have you know that these little things are chockfull of vitamin C and fiber, and are really good for your health."

Kyle chuckled. "I'm not saying they aren't, just that I need something more meaty or I'll starve to death. Do you want me to starve to death?"

Logan was about to answer when his eyes drifted away, to somewhere behind Kyle. Kyle turned round and saw a middle-aged man walking towards them, smiling, with a stance like he could take on the world. His hair and beard were greying and his chiseled face sported a growing network of wrinkles, especially around his brown eyes. The man was probably in his mid-fifties, but was big and seemed strong enough to knock down either one of them if necessary.

"Logan," the man said, reaching for his hand, his smile widening.

Logan seemed shocked to see him here but quickly recovered and smiled back. "Dave. What are you doing here?" he said, shaking the man's hand.

"Oh, you know, buying some stuff to enjoy over the weekend. But actually, it's good I've run into you here. I needed to talk to you about something." Dave paused and glanced at Kyle. He seemed unsure of saying whatever it was he wanted to say.

"Dave, this is Kyle," Logan said.

"Nice to meet you," Dave said, shaking Kyle's hand.

"What was it you needed to talk about?" Logan seemed unsure.

Dave turned back to Logan. "I was going to call you. I'm retiring, so I won't be working with you anymore."

Logan's mouth fell open and Kyle could swear he had lost a bit of color, despite the heat.

"What? Really? Why? What happened?" Logan asked in an anxious tone.

Dave chuckled. "Well, you know how these things are. There comes a time when your body starts playing tricks on you and you find yourself not being able to do what you used to."

"Come on. You seem perfectly in shape to me," Logan said, raising one hand dismissively and trying to smile. Kyle thought he seemed more frightened than playful, though.

"That's what I think too, but my doctor says I need to settle down. The good old ticker has starting complaining lately."

Logan's shoulders fell. "My god, Dave, I'm so sorry. Are you okay?"

Dave chuckled again. "Don't give me that look. I'm not dead yet. With what modern medicine can do, I'll bet you I'll still be around for another fifty years. Well, provided my insurance company pays what they're supposed to. But I digress." Dave paused, shifted his weight to the other leg and glanced at Kyle again. "Anyway, I just wanted to say how it's been a pleasure working with you. You're a great guy, with lots of potential. I wish all the guys I worked with were like you. Don't ever forget it."

Logan nodded but said nothing. Dave then said, "You'll be contacted by someone soon. I'll do everything in my power to make sure they choose someone you can trust, okay?"

"Thanks, Dave. It means a lot to me."

"Ah, come here." Dave reached out his arms and pulled Logan closer, hugging him in his bear-like grip, patting Logan on the back, shaking him with every bang.

"This isn't the last you'll be hearing of me. I'll be in touch. I promise."

With that, Dave shook Kyle's hand as well and left. Logan stared after him as he walked down the aisle, sadness blooming in his eyes.

"Who was that?"

Logan seemed to wake up from a trance and looked at Kyle. "An old friend."

"Oh? You used to work together?"

Logan smiled. "Kind of. Do you have everything? Are you ready to go?"

Kyle was now very aware that every time he asked Logan about his life, his answers were always sparse on details.

"Is he a former boyfriend?"

Logan chuckled. "What? God, no. He's a friend, not boyfriend. Why did you think he was?"

Kyle shrugged. "Every time I try to talk with you about your life you kind of avoid it. You're always scant on details and I end up knowing as much as I did before asking. Take Dave, there. I know you said he's a friend, but how did you meet him? Why was he talking to you like that, almost as if there was something he didn't want me to hear? Where did you work together? Who is this person who'll replace him and why would he talk to you about it? There are so many questions I have right now and the only thing I know is that he's a 'friend'. I'm trying to be cool about us and our relationship, you know, but it's a bit hard when I feel you don't give back as much as I give. For example, whenever I ask you about your family, where you're from or what you did before coming here, you never answer."

Logan chuckled but seemed nervous. "You say it like I'm hiding something from you."

"Are you?"

Logan gazed at Kyle for a couple of seconds. "You can relax. I'm not a serial killer with dead bodies in my basement."

"That's not what I asked."

Logan sighed. "If you really want to know, the reason I don't speak about my family is because I don't know who my father is and my mother was a drunk who constantly changed boyfriends and looked at me like I was a burden in her life."

Kyle raised his eyebrows, feeling the air escaping him. "I'm… I'm so sorry. I didn't know."

"You don't have to be sorry. It is what it is. And you didn't know about any of this stuff. But you understand now why I don't like to talk about it?"

Kyle pursed his lips and hugged Logan with his free arm. "I'm so sorry," he said after stepping back.

"Don't be. Can we forget about this and go away to our weekend?"

***

Logan felt terrible for not telling Kyle the whole truth. He told himself that the shock of having Dave telling him he wouldn't be his parole officer anymore prevented him from having the guts to tell Kyle the whole story. He'd tell him everything as soon as they were settled in the cabin. Logan just needed a moment to gather himself and collect his thoughts. For now, he was just relieved the story about his parents had deflected Kyle's attention.

As they drove out of town, Logan thought of Dave. He'd been pivotal in his life. Logan had expected him to be another disappointment, another someone looking at him like the felon he used to be, counting the days until he'd be behind bars again. But Dave was nothing of the sort. He'd made it abundantly clear that he was there to help him in whatever he needed. He'd been the one who'd advised him on the shelter that had helped Logan take his first steps outside the only house he'd known for the previous five years. Dave always said he wanted to help Logan become of the person he knew he was, and that had made a world of difference. When nobody else believed in him, not even himself, Dave was there to remind him he didn't need to be another failure in the penal system. He had his whole life ahead of him and Dave would make sure he stayed firmly on the right path.

Logan eventually stopped the car in front of a wooden cabin he'd used once before. His boss had been the one to tell him about it a couple of months before, after arriving all smiles and happy from a three-day retreat in heaven, as he'd put it. And although Logan had never been away before, much less on his own, Mr. Shaffer had persuaded him to try and rent the cabin for a weekend after saying he was too tense about work. So, after a weekend away, he'd returned relaxed and thankful for having taken his boss's advice.

"Wow. This place is beautiful," Kyle said, immediately he'd stepped out of the truck and looked around.

It truly was. There was nothing around for miles but trees, the dirt road the only clue they were still fairly nearby modern civilization. The cabin itself was all wood, with only one floor and a small porch from which they could enjoy the scenery set out below. It was perched on top of a small hill and right below a river meandered through a forest that stretched as far as the eye could see. A large, old oak tree grew behind it and stretched its branches over the roof, almost as if embracing the house. It seemed something out of a fairy tale.

"You like it?" Logan asked, grinning.

Kyle took his phone out and looked at its screen as he took a picture. After he was finished, he kept looking at the screen as he waved his arm around, from one position to another. "I do like it, but we don't have reception here."

"That's the whole point."

"But I'm expecting a call from my client."

Logan approached Kyle and kissed him. "Relax and forget about your client. He's not going anywhere. You're supposed to enjoy yourself, remember? And it is the weekend."

"You're right. I guess it's moments like these that show you how hooked you are."

Logan chuckled. "You mean, how hooked you are."

"Yes, I confess. I can't live without my phone. Now stop rubbing your feature phone in other people's faces and how you're not into twenty-first century gadgets," Kyle said with a laugh.

After settling in, they went for a walk but soon returned. It was getting dark fast. The tree canopy was thick and shrouded the place in shadows. The temperature was also much lower than in Greenville, which caught them by surprise. They hadn't packed warm clothing as summer was in full force when they'd left town.

Logan lit the fire in the living room as soon as they got back and Kyle went searching for one of the bottles of red wine they had brought along.

"Ah, this is much better," Kyle said after sitting beside Logan on a thick, fluffy rug in front of the fireplace. He offered Logan one of the glasses of wine he was carrying.

"I'm thinking we're gonna be too hot in a couple of minutes," Logan said, taking his glass of wine.

"Are you kidding me? I'm freezing after that walk."

Logan took a sip of wine. In his mind, he was telling himself he should speak to Kyle and tell him everything about his past, but couldn't quite bring himself to do it. He didn't want to ruin the moment nor the weekend but, above all else, he feared Kyle's reaction. He could only think of how, in his interviews, people had looked at him differently after realizing he'd been in prison. And although he hoped Kyle was different, he feared it was too soon to find out.

"What are you thinking about?"

Logan snapped out of his musings. Kyle was looking at him with lovely eyes and a sweet smile. "How great it is to be here with you," he ended up saying, feeling terrible about his white lie.

Chapter Sixteen

Logan woke up screaming. He didn't know where he was and that added to the terror of the nightmare.

"Shh, it's okay. It was a bad dream," Kyle was saying, stroking Logan's arm.

Kyle's voice grounded him and it all came back to Logan: the weekend away, the cabin. He drew in a ragged breath and allowed himself to relax. It had been almost a month since his last nightmare. He'd almost got used to the idea that they were gone for good.

"What time is it?" Logan asked, trying to ignore his lingering sense of dread.

"Seven a.m. What were you dreaming about?"

Logan puffed his cheeks out and let go of the air in a long and noisy exhale. "It's weird but I don't remember anymore," he lied. The prison walls closing in on him were still vividly scarred on his memory, but he couldn't tell Kyle about it. At least, not yet.

"It's so annoying when that happens," Kyle said. "Why is it that dreams slip away from our grasp so quickly and we're left with just a feeling?"

Logan closed his eyes. "I don't know. What I do know is that it's too early to be having philosophical conversations." He snored loudly and pretended to be asleep.

"Oh, oh. Really classy of you."

Logan pushed the sheets away from them and straddled Kyle, then kissed him. "How about we move up our schedule and go to that place I told you about yesterday?"

"Can we have breakfast first? Or at least brush our teeth? Morning breath!" Kyle pinched his nose and gagged.

"Shut up!"

***

"The weather just doesn't know what it wants, now does it?" Kyle said, wiping his sweaty forehead with the back of his hand.

Logan looked over his shoulder. "You were the one complaining about how cold it was last night. Maybe it heard you," and he chuckled.

"Haha. Funny."

The day had dawned hot, without so much as a hint of a breeze. After a quick breakfast, they'd gone for a walk and were now sweating profusely. Logan wanted to show Kyle a small waterfall nearby, one he'd discovered during his first time here.

"The place is worth it. You'll see," Logan said, resuming walking.

"I hope so because I can't keep walking much more. I thought I was in shape. I really did. But I'm not."

Logan smiled. It was endearing to see a fully-grown man trying to keep up with him. "Save your breath. We still have another hill to go before arriving at the waterfall."

They kept walking for ten more minutes in silence, save for Kyle's labored breathing. Logan was still thinking on whether or not he should tell him the whole truth about his past, but every minute that ticked by buried that need deeper and deeper. Why ruin the weekend? They were both happy and getting along, and Logan had already told him about his parents. It wasn't everything about himself, but it was something, right?

"We're almost there," Logan said.

They had reached the summit of the small hill they'd been climbing. They couldn't see it yet on account of all the trees and ferns, but five hundred feet away the river fell into a small pool and the sound was unmistakable.

"I can hear it," Kyle said, smiling and sounding relieved.

They walked the last couple hundred feet to the base of the waterfall with renewed energy. The water fell twenty, maybe twenty-five feet from above before crashing into the pool and then flowing out along the river's continued course. Around the pool was a small cove, leafy and secluded.

Kyle let his backpack fall to the pebbly ground, a look of wonder in his eyes. Logan mimicked him. It felt like they were the only people in the world.

"You like it?" Logan asked.

Kyle scanned the place, trying to catch his breath. "Seems like you were right. This was worth the walk."

"And you know what's really fun to do around here?"

Kyle silently shook his head in query, to which Logan grinned and slid off his T-shirt and shorts. He ran into the pool wearing nothing but his swimming trunks and then dived into its crystal clear water.

"Come on!" he shouted, after returning to the surface and shaking the excess water off his hair.

There was no need to insist, though. Kyle was already getting out of his clothes. He ran in Logan's direction and cannonballed into the water, splashing it everywhere.

"The water's amazing," Kyle said, a moment later.

"I'd say the water's freezing but it helps we're so hot."

Kyle scoffed. "You're so full of yourself," he said, making fun of him. He splashed water onto Logan's face who tried, unsuccessfully, to avoid it.

"I didn't mean it that way. I was talking about the heat," Logan protested. Kyle laughed and splashed him again. "Oh, now you're in big trouble."

Logan swam towards Kyle, who retreated by swimming towards the waterfall, his powerful strokes pushing him along. Logan was momentarily taken aback by his speed. Damn, he's fast. He put away that thought and put more effort into his own strokes, trying to shorten the distance between them. A moment later, he reached him. They were now behind the waterfall, in a small recess in the rock. Kyle splashed him again.

"Will you stop that?" Logan said, grabbing Kyle's hands.

"Make me."

The mischievous grin dancing on Kyle's lips didn't go unnoticed. Around them, the rock was painted with the iridescent glow of the sunlight. The world outside disappeared and went mute as Logan kissed him. Nothing else mattered. His past, what he should tell him, Dave… They were all insignificant details in the grand scheme of things.

Logan leaned back, still holding Kyle by the small of his back. Kyle looked flushed, his eyes unfocused. Logan smiled. "Will you stop, now?"

Kyle nodded and grinned. "You've earned it."

Logan pulled him closer and kissed him again. There was a noticeable volume swelling in Kyle's groin, pressing against Logan's crotch. His penis reacted promptly, tenting under his swimming trunks. He grabbed Kyle harder and ground his penis against Kyle's, feeling the heat that came from his throbbing cock.

"Wait," Kyle said, pulling away from Logan. He was panting and flushed.

"Is there something wrong?" Logan's chest was rising and falling to the rhythm of his passion.

"I… I can't. I want to, I really, really want to, but I can't. It's like there's this wall I can't go around that makes me nauseated. I'm sorry."

Logan tried to pace his breathing. "You've nothing to be sorry about. I was being too intense."

"I really want you."

"I know. I could feel it," Logan said, chuckling and trying to lighten the mood.

Kyle frowned, pretending to be offended, and splashed his face with water. He then swam away, laughing like he'd done something hilarious.

105

"Oh, you're so in trouble, now!" Logan said, going after him.

***

The day went by quickly. Logan found himself thinking of how he had never felt so close to anyone and how good it felt. It was easy to be with Kyle and talk with him, and the hours flew by without either of them noticing. The heat of that day faded into a brisk evening. They arrived at the cabin just before sunset, around the time the wind picked up and the temperature fell. They were both starving, and after a quick shower, Logan lit the fire and prepared a couple of sandwiches.

"This is the best sandwich I've ever had," Kyle said, his eyes beaming.

Logan came in from the kitchenette with another plate of sandwiches, which he placed on the little table in front of the couch. Then he sat by Kyle's side. "I'm glad you like it because that right there is dinner," and he pointed at the plate he'd just placed on the table.

"You could be a chef."

"What?"

"A sandwich chef." Kyle laughed at his own joke.

"I can already see me traveling the country and selling sandwiches. Seems like a dream come true."

"It could happen."

"Naturally."

Kyle chewed on another bite. He seemed to be reflecting on something as his eyes drifted away from Logan. He blinked and again focused on him. "But seriously, do you ever think about the future? I mean, what do you see yourself doing in five years?"

That was a really good question, one to which Logan didn't have an answer. He'd been focusing only on the present.

"I really don't know. Building furniture, I guess."

"In your own company?"

Logan shrugged. "I don't know. I don't think it's ever occurred to me to have my own business."

"I think you'd be great at it. Think about it. You could build your own stuff and sell it at a huge profit instead of working your ass off for someone else. I could help you with your branding. If you ever think about it, I'll come up with your company logo."

Logan smiled. Kyle's enthusiasm was palpable. "That's actually not a bad idea."

"Of course it's not."

"You have a deal." Logan winked and sipped on his wine. "And how about you?"

"What about me?"

"Do you see yourself living in Greenville?"

Kyle nodded. "Totally. I never imagined myself living in a small town, much less Greenville. I used to think of this place as somewhere no one cared about. I even wanted to sell the house, but now I'm glad I didn't. These last few weeks have shown me how happy I can be in a place like this." He stroked Logan's thigh and smiled in a tender way.

"Is that so?" Logan grabbed Kyle's arm and gently pulled him closer. Kyle rested his back against Logan's chest and snuggled there, as if building a small nest for himself.

"I could get used to this."

Logan chuckled. "You mean me hugging you? Eating sandwiches?"

"That, yes, and being with you, daydreaming about the future—our future."

Logan tilted his head. "Really? That's mighty forward coming from someone who wasn't sure we should have come here for the weekend."

"Well, it's your fault for making me feel so comfortable around you."

Logan hugged him tighter. Kyle turned back and he kissed him. He wanted to say something nice, something that showed Kyle he was thrilled to know he was thinking about a future together, but felt guilty. Right now, he could only think about his own past.

Chapter Seventeen

Logan got up early the next morning. It was their last day there and he wanted to make Kyle some breakfast. Scrambled eggs with bacon and coffee was just what the doctor had ordered. He was finishing setting the plates when he heard feet dragging along the floor. He turned and saw a groggy Kyle rubbing his eyes and yawning.

"Morning, sleepyhead."

Kyle stretched. "Morning. That smells good."

Logan held him by the small of his back and kissed him tenderly. "And it tastes even better. You want some coffee now? You seem like you need some in you". Kyle nodded and Logan chuckled. "I think you're still asleep."

"I think I am."

Kyle dragged himself to the couch and Logan brought him a cup of the steamy, dark liquid. Its aroma had a jumpstart effect on Kyle, who seemed to waken up with a start.

"Thank you," he said while sipping the hot coffee.

"I thought we could go for a walk before heading out into town."

"Sounds like a plan. But I have to drink this first. And have a shower. I'm still sleepy."

Logan laughed. "I can see that. Didn't you sleep well?"

"I did. I'm just tired from yesterday."

"You mean trekking to the waterfall and swimming for a bit?" Kyle nodded and Logan added: "Man, you're in bad shape. But don't worry, 'cuz my breakfast will wake you up. And if that doesn't do it, I can think of a couple other things we could try to wake you up." Logan winked in an exaggerated way and Kyle almost choked on his coffee after his fit of laughter.

***

Their morning walk stoked their appetites. Kyle was telling Logan about his love for pizza and they ended up going to the nearby town to have some for lunch before returning to Greenville. It wasn't part of their plans, but all that talk had left them with a yearning for the Italian dish. They had just parked right beside where all the restaurants seem to be when Logan saw someone who made him pause.

"Is everything okay?" Kyle asked.

Logan glanced at him, going through his options, but it was too late to head back. "That's one of my bosses," he said, in a whisper. Sean Hamilton had already seen him and, as always, didn't seem too happy about it. He was walking in their direction with a woman. Logan had never seen her before, but they seemed to be together.

"What are you doing here?" Mr. Hamilton said, looking at him from under a heavy frown. Logan knew right there and then that he wouldn't be too thrilled if he found out who Kyle was.

The woman squeezed his arm. "Sean! Where are your manners?"

Mr. Hamilton grumbled something under his breath. "Caroline, this is one of my employees."

One of his employees. Apparently, he wasn't worthy of having a name.

"I'm Logan. Nice to meet you."

"Nice to meet you, too. And please excuse my husband's mood. He seems to be having a hard time forgetting about work, although we're supposed to be having fun." She laughed, trying to pass her remark off as a joke, but Logan wasn't sure admonishing Mr. Hamilton in public would help her any.

Caroline turned to Kyle and scanned him from head to toe. "And who is this dashing young man?"

Logan held his breath. He'd never addressed his sexuality with his bosses before and wasn't sure how they would react. He was pretty sure Mr. Shaffer wouldn't have a problem with it but Mr. Hamilton was a different matter.

"This is Kyle. We spent the weekend nearby. It's a lovely area." He decided to confront the problem head on. Logan was more worried that there was a small chance of Mr. Hamilton realizing Kyle was a client. He most likely wouldn't, as he wasn't in the store the first time Kyle had stopped by, but Logan couldn't be sure.

"You make such an adorable couple. Don't you think, Sean?"

Caroline's hands were crossed over her heart and she was smiling, like she'd just seen a litter of newborn puppies. Mr. Hamilton, on the other hand, didn't seem to share her enthusiasm.

"We're gonna be late, Caroline." With that, Mr. Hamilton nodded and they left.

Logan watched them leave, his stomach churning. His boss hadn't seemed too pleased. Logan wasn't sure if it was just his normal unsympathetic personality bubbling to the surface or something else.

"He didn't seem very nice. Is he always like that?" Kyle said, a moment later.

"He is. Fortunately, he doesn't spend too much time in the store. He's always traveling," Logan said, still watching as his boss walked down the street with his wife.

"I don't know why but I got the feeling he wasn't happy with us. Do you think he's got a problem with...you know?"

"What? Gays?"

"Yeah."

Logan shrugged. "I don't know. It's not a subject we've talked about before."

So Kyle had noticed it too. Should he be worried this could impact his job? Mr. Hamilton had never liked him much, but now it seemed he had something specific to dislike him for. Beyond his past as a criminal, that is. Logan sighed. Even if it were true, Mr. Shaffer would never let something like Logan's sexuality influence him.

"Maybe I'm just seeing homophobes everywhere because this is all new to me."

Logan watched as Kyle waved his hand, as if talking about them. "You feel exposed?"

"A bit, yes."

"You've nothing to fear. I'm here with you." Kyle's eyes smiled and warmed Logan's heart. "How about we go get that pizza?"

They headed out to the pizzeria. Logan hoped bumping into his grumpy boss wouldn't cause him trouble. He needed the job. He didn't want to go through the hell of trying to find someone else willing to employ an ex-convict. He still recalled all too vividly what that had been like. Logan shook his head and tried to bury his worries. He wanted to enjoy this last meal with Kyle before heading back home. He could worry then.

***

Logan pulled the truck up by Kyle's driveway. It was late afternoon and the trip home had gone by too quickly even though Logan had driven lazily so they could enjoy the scenery. He was already missing their time together which, up until his boss showing up, had been nothing short of perfect. The road trip and the ease with which time seemed to fly by when he was with Kyle made the grumpy man all but a distant memory, though.

"Thank you for a lovely weekend," Kyle said, after having kissed Logan.

"You don't have to thank me," Logan said with a smile.

"I know. I just wanted you to know . Wanna come up?"

"I'd love to, but I have to go get Buddy. I don't want him annoying Mrs. Cook tonight as well."

Kyle kissed him again. "See you tomorrow?

"See you tomorrow."

Logan drove off, nostalgia kicking into high gear. The weekend had been too short. And this first experience of being with someone, of being part of a couple, was something he could get used to.

Chapter Eighteen

"Well, I'm finally done here."

Logan looked around Ryan's bedroom. It was probably one of his best works to date. Every piece of furniture screamed cuteness overload because of its tiny size.

"It's beautiful," Kyle said. "But does this mean I'll only see you after work from now on?"

Logan chuckled. "Well, yeah. What do you think? I spend my days roaming around other people's houses?"

"I hope not. Just mine."

Kyle smiled. Logan approached and kissed him. "At least now I won't feel like I'm doing something hugely inappropriate. You'll be just my guy. Not my client."

Kyle laughed. "Yeah, that sounds hugely inappropriate."

"You know what? I think you should call Jessica. Tell her about the finished room. Ask her to come up here again. I think it'd be a good opportunity for you guys to sort things out, now that the house is finally becoming a home," Logan said as they walked out of the room.

Kyle shrugged. "Maybe. I don't know. She's been silent since we last spoke. But I'll call her and see if I manage to convince her."

Logan pecked his lips. "Tell me how it goes afterwards. I have to go. See you this evening?"

Logan drove off to town, feeling a sense of accomplishment. His first project was finally finished and he was proud of it.

Mr. Shaffer would be pleased with the result. He was certain of it. And he needed every bit of approval he could muster from his boss right now. He'd spent the past few days since his weekend with Kyle fearing Mr. Hamilton would appear in the shop, accusing him of dating clients and dragging the company's name through the mud. Logan had been jumpy ever since. Of course, his rational self knew Mr. Hamilton didn't know who Kyle was and so wouldn't know to accuse him of dating clients. But still. So, he went into Mr. Shaffer's office as soon as he arrived at Shaffer & Hamilton Woodworks. Logan was excited to give his boss the good news about the completion of his first work flying solo.

"Do you have a minute?" he asked, after knocking and opening the door.

Mr. Shaffer was behind his desk, nose deep into a stack of papers. "Come in but you'll have to be quick. These buying orders are driving me crazy," Mr. Shaffer said, raising a handful of sheets of paper.

"I just wanted to report that I've finished that project at Mr. Seddon's. Here are some pictures." Logan whipped his phone out and showed them to his boss.

"Well, congratulations. This looks really good."

Logan's chest swelled up with pride. "Thanks, Mr. Shaffer."

"It's a shame that phone of yours has a lousy screen, though. I can barely make any of the details, but I think it'd be great to have that furniture in our portfolio. Could you ask Mr. Seddon for some pictures, maybe?"

"Of course."

"Good. When you're done, talk to Mike. There's a new project coming in and it's yours."

Logan's grin was impossible to control. Not only was his boss happy with his work but he was giving him another project to work on, all by himself. It was a bit ridiculous to fear he could be demoted, but the thought had been on his mind for a while.

"Thanks, Mr. Shaffer." He left the office believing he could take on the world.

***

Kyle got out of his car at Shaffer & Hamilton Woodworks and headed into the store. Logan had called with the exciting news and he'd decided to go personally and give Mr. Shaffer the pictures. He would put in a good word for Logan as well and so cement the idea that he was a wonderful employee with his boss.

The shop had a couple of people browsing and a nice-looking employee overseeing the place, his hands behind his back. He smiled as soon as he saw Kyle come in and came to meet him.

"Good afternoon. Can I help you?"

"Hi. I'm looking for Mr. Shaffer. Is he in?"

The man seemed hesitant, but after Kyle explained why he was there, he broke into a big smile, asked Kyle to wait and went looking for his boss. A couple of minutes later, Kyle was being shown into Mr. Shaffer's office.

"Mr. Seddon. What a surprise. Thank you for coming in but it really wasn't necessary. You could've just sent the photos by email. Please," and he gestured Kyle to sit down.

Kyle shook his hand and sat on one of the two chairs in front of Mr. Shaffer's desk. "I could've, but my internet connection is awfully slow. It's easier and faster this way."

"I could've sent someone to pick them up."

"It's no trouble, really. This way I get to tell you in person how happy I am with Logan's work. He's really professional and I'm only sorry I don't need any more furniture. I'd hire you guys in a heartbeat."

Mr. Shaffer chuckled. "I'm happy to hear it."

Kyle was just preparing another witty remark about the good job Logan had done when a man entered the office. Kyle recognized the face but couldn't place from where. But then, the grumpy expression set off an alarm somewhere deep inside his mind and Kyle went pale.

"Sean. Back so soon?" Mr. Shaffer was sporting a smile that wasn't being reciprocated. The man, who Kyle now recognized as the grumpy boss he and Logan had bumped into during their weekend, was staring at him with a confused expression. Mr. Shaffer continued: "This is Mr. Seddon, a client. He was just telling me how happy he is with Logan's work."

Kyle felt the blood in his face get sucked deeper inside him. The man, Sean, turned to Mr. Shaffer with a shocked expression, and then back at Kyle.

"Is that so? Well, I can certainly say I'm not surprised."

Kyle had not thought his impromptu visit through. In his desire to help Logan impress his boss, he'd completely forgotten about the risk of running into his other boss. He smiled tentatively and said, "Here are the photos. I hope they're good enough for your portfolio." He gave Mr. Shaffer a pen drive and tried to maintain a sense of dignity he wasn't feeling.

"I'm sorry to be rude, but could you excuse us? I have an important matter to discuss with my partner," the grumpy boss said, looking at Kyle.

"Certainly." Kyle smiled tentatively again and left, after saying goodbye to the two men.

As soon as he left the store, he dialed Logan's number. He had to warn him. Logan didn't even know he was here. Kyle had meant it as a surprise but the whole thing now looked like it might turn into a very different kind of surprise.

Logan didn't pick up and the call went straight voicemail.

"Ah… It's me. I meant this as a surprise but I came by your work to give Mr. Shaffer the pictures I took of Ryan's room, and to talk you up to him. But I ran into your grumpy boss and I'm almost sure he recognized me. I'm sorry. I didn't think this through."

Kyle hung up, still dazed. He just hoped Logan wouldn't get into in trouble over it.

***

Logan had just arrived from the wood warehouse at the back of the workshop. He was looking at the notes Mike had given him about a new project when he thought he heard someone yelling. He looked up and his stomach sank. The window blinds on his boss's office were not entirely closed as they usually were, and he noticed his two bosses seemingly arguing. Mr. Shaffer was sitting behind his desk but Mr. Hamilton was standing and gesticulating with wide movements. He seemed angry about something. Could their argument have something to do with the weekend? It couldn't be, though. Mr. Hamilton had no idea who Kyle was.

He returned to his work but with a bad feeling pressing down on his stomach. A couple of minutes later, he heard the door to Mr. Shaffer's office opening and closing. Mr. Hamilton, his grumpy boss, walked by without even acknowledging him.

"Logan? Can you come in here for a minute?"

Logan's eyes drifted away from Mr. Hamilton to Mr. Shaffer who was by his office door, looking at him. He nodded and went in.

Mr. Shaffer closed the door behind them. "Please, sit."

Logan did as asked. His boss seemed upset. "Is there something wrong?"

Mr. Shaffer looked at him and sighed. "Sean told me you're dating a client." Mr. Shaffer paused and Logan felt his stomach sink. How the hell did he know? Logan opened his mouth to say something, to defend himself, but there was no defense. It was true. Before he could articulate a single sound, however, Mr. Shaffer continued: "It's not our policy to meddle in our employees' private lives, and I couldn't care less if you're interested in dating men or women. What we don't condone is dating clients, as that can be... Well, awkward? I don't even know how to put it as it's never happened before. At least, not that I know of." Mr. Shaffer was now scratching his head. "The thing is, Logan, Sean is worried that you dating a client can send...the wrong message about the company. The good news, I suppose, is that the work at Mr. Seddon's is done and so this isn't a problem anymore."

"I don't know what to say. I'm sorry for letting this happen, Mr. Shaffer, but I can assure you I didn't take this step lightly. I… I spent a good chunk of time avoiding…avoiding my feelings because I knew it was inappropriate. I've let you down and I really don't know how I can make it up to you." Logan now felt he'd betrayed the only man who had given him a second chance.

Mr. Shaffer chuckled. "Now, now, it's not the end of the world. At least, not for me. Sean thinks this is something that should warrant your demotion at least, although he's more inclined to fire you. But I don't share his view on this."

"Thank you, Mr. Shaffer. I really appreciate it."

Mr. Shaffer smiled and leaned over the table. "You could've talked to me about this, you know. Had you been honest with me about your feelings I could've helped you avoid this mess. Promise me the next time you'll come to me first. And avoid running into Sean, for that matter."

His boss winked and Logan realized he was trying to lighten the mood. "I can promise you this won't happen again."

Logan left the office, itching to call Kyle or send him a message to tell him what had happened. But he couldn't. Not after almost losing his job. He didn't want to push his luck, so he went straight to work and didn't notice Kyle's voicemail until much later.

***

Logan arrived at Kyle's that evening relieved for not having to hide his relationship at work anymore. Having his boss talk to him about it had almost given him a heart attack, but now that the cat was out of the bag it was one less thing he had to worry about.

"I'm so, so sorry. I should never have gone there. I just wanted to talk you up to your boss. It never occurred to me

119

that grumpy guy would be there," Kyle said as soon as Logan had closed the door behind him.

"What's done is done."

"Was it bad?"

"Not as much as I'd feared. Mr. Shaffer basically told me that, although Mr. Hamilton was really angry, there would be no consequences at all. He just asked me not to make the same mistake and run into Grumpy next time I decide to date a client," Logan said as they walked into the living room.

Kyle squinted. "Next time?"

"Didn't you know? This is my thing. I seduce clients all the time." Logan chuckled. "I told him there wouldn't be a next time, obviously."

"For a moment there I thought I'd be shooing guys away from you from now on."

Logan laughed. "What do you take me for? Some kind of guy whisperer?"

"I really hope not."

Logan approached Kyle and kissed him, pushing him onto the couch. They landed on the cushions still kissing and Logan gripped Kyle harder, a wave of desire rushing through him. Maybe it came from being happy that everything at last seemed to be falling into place, or maybe that endless kissing that had led nowhere, but he was now ready to take on Kyle right here on the couch. He forced himself to stop and leaned back. After a couple of deep breaths his rational mind was again in control.

"Did you call Jessica?" he said, trying to put his desire to one side.

Kyle blushed and looked feverish. He ran his fingers through his hair, as if trying to compose himself. Logan took a deep breath to keep his desire calmed. He knew Kyle wasn't ready for the next step and that waiting was the right thing to do.

"I did and she said she'd think about it. If I'm honest, I'm getting anxious about this whole thing. I miss Ryan and I want to have him with me. I'm more than ready. I don't want him to forget me."

"He won't. And don't give up. Call her again tomorrow if necessary. Tell her you have a right to see your son."

Kyle smiled. "Thanks for being so understanding and patient."

Logan shrugged. "You're worth the wait."

Chapter Nineteen

Kyle was driving to Logan's, his windows open, the pine scents of that late afternoon summer's day wafting around him. The past few weeks had been surreal. He was with a man, and a gorgeous one at that, but at the same time he felt somewhat detached, as if he were watching someone else in his place. He tried not to think too much about it and just enjoy this new chapter of his life to the fullest. This feeling was probably only due to him knowing, deep down, that it still seemed like he was doing something wrong. But he wasn't, and Logan had been nothing but patient and wonderful with him. The only problem was that their kissing sessions were getting longer and hotter, and they'd be both out of breath by the end of them. The first time Kyle felt Logan's erection pressing against him, his heart had galloped away and rapped against his ribcage like crazy, leaving him panting as his body went into overdrive. It felt very much like being a teenager again, discovering his own sexuality for the first time, the stimulus too much to bear.

This horniness had been slowly charging up since their weekend in the cabin, but at the same time he felt anxious about taking the next step. The thought of ripping Logan's clothes off and having sex with him always ended up in palpitations and a queasy stomach. Kyle thought it was related to this idea he had that somehow he wouldn't be able to satisfy Logan. It was silly and immature of him to think that way, of course. They were two adults perfectly capable of communicating with each other. Plus, Logan had been clear about sex being whatever made him comfortable and not what he thought he was supposed to do.

What he really needed to do was stop overthinking things and get out of his own head. Kyle didn't know how much more of the dry humping he would be able to endure, though. He'd been walking around for the past few days with a tingling sensation on his skin that never really went away, a crackling electricity that wouldn't let him think clearly. He needed to do something about it, and that something clearly involved a very naked Logan wrapped around him.

Kyle shuddered at the thought and his penis came alive, pressing itself against his jeans and leaking heat into his thigh. He sighed raggedly as he pulled up on Logan's driveway. That would have to wait. They were going to the movies after dinner, to celebrate Ryan's finished room, and he was really looking forward to it. The idea of having sex with Logan, though, still throbbed at the back of his mind.

"Logan?" Kyle said as he stepped into the house. Buddy yapped and came running, his tail wagging. "Hey, Buddy. How are you? Hmm? You good?" Buddy was on his hind legs, leaning on Kyle who now squatted to rub Buddy's ears. "Who's a good boy? Who's a good boy?"

"Don't mind me," Logan said, coming out of the kitchen and grinning at the sight of Kyle addressing Buddy in baby talk.

"He's so cute. I can't help it," Kyle said, standing up.

"Oh yeah? Cuter than I am?"

Kyle chuckled. "He's definitely much cuter that you, yes."

Logan, who by now was only an inch away from Kyle, grabbed him by the small of his back and kissed him tenderly. Kyle felt his penis waking up again throbbing against his leg.

Logan parted lips with him. "Well, hello, sir," he said, a mischievous grin on his lips.

Kyle chuckled, embarrassed. "Sorry, but I can't control it."

"It's flattering to know I have this effect on you." Logan paused, gazing at him, a warm smile dancing on his lips. He seemed about to say something but then appeared to change his mind and closed his mouth. "Should we go?"

Kyle wanted to say he'd prefer staying in but ended up nodding.

They left, Logan promising Buddy he wouldn't be long, and went to Kyle's SUV, merrily chatting about something that had happened at Logan's work that day. Kyle tried his best to listen and comment where appropriate but his mind was somewhere else.

"Are you okay?" Logan asked a couple of minutes after they'd left, placing his hand on Kyle's thigh.

Kyle's heart galloped away at the touch, there, precisely on top of his engorged penis. Logan's gesture had been innocent enough. He had no way of knowing that Kyle's blooming erection was making it hard for him to think about anything else than a naked Logan. But now he'd almost certainly be aware of it. There was no way he couldn't feel it.

He peeked at Logan and was about to say something when Logan squeezed the shape of Kyle's penis. It throbbed into a full-blown erection that soon became uncomfortably tight. His jeans didn't have much room in them when he was sitting and things were a lot more cramped in his current state.

"It's just that I…I need you," Kyle said, swallowing hard, "but I'm not sure I'm ready."

Logan squeezed his penis again and Kyle whimpered.

"How about we take a detour to your place and see what happens? We won't do anything you don't want to."

Logan's voice was husky and his hand sizzling hot. Kyle peeked again at him and decided the movie could wait. There were more pressing matters at hand.

Kyle made a turn to his house as soon as he could, his heart drumming in his ears. He was nervous about what was about to happen but felt he couldn't wait any longer. He was ready for this—he had to be.

They arrived at Kyle's house a couple of minutes later. He killed the engine and turned to Logan, lips ajar and breathing fast. Logan leaned in and kissed him, his tongue exploring his mouth while his hand stroked his penis. A jolt of lust spread through him and he grabbed Logan's hand. He leaned back and inhaled sharply through his teeth.

"Please stop."

"Don't you like it?" Logan asked, looking like he felt sorry.

"No, it's not that." Kyle paused, embarrassed to admit what was really happening. "It's… If you continue doing that, I'm gonna… I'm gonna come," he said, almost whispering.

Logan smiled. "My first time with a guy I didn't last five minutes. I was so anxious, so horny and excited that it all ended way too fast. Don't worry."

Kyle felt himself relaxing a bit. "Let's go inside."

Logan nodded. The day was quickly coming to an end, a warm breeze blowing from the west. Kyle felt too hot in his own skin. He wasn't sure if it was from the heat or the adrenaline rushing through his body.

As they walked inside, Logan grabbed Kyle by the small of his back, soon grinding on his crotch. He leaned in and kissed him, and Kyle felt his bones melting away into a puddle of jelly. Logan gently pushed him towards the living room, grabbing him by his waist. There, he slid Kyle's T-shirt over his head and kissed his nipples just as Kyle was about to lower his arms. Logan then kissed him on his abs and kept going down, until he reached his jeans. He unzipped and pushed them down, along with his boxer shorts. Kyle's cock bounced up, throbbing and engorged, and Logan licked it from its base to its tip, making his way slowly up. Kyle gasped and shuddered at the wet feeling, his mind focusing on the typhoon of emotions now rushing through him. It all felt like a dream, a very vivid one where his heart beat so fast it threatened to pull itself away. Logan kept licking his cock, slowly, taking his time lapping on its crown. Logan took him into his mouth and Kyle's hands balled into fists while Logan sucked him, his tongue quickly swirling around the tip every time he came up. Kyle looked down and placed his hands on Logan's head as the most exquisite sensation he'd ever felt grew inside him, a radiant heat that made him reverberate with pleasure. The pressure grew and his rational self realized what was about to happen.

"I'm gonna come," he cried, and Logan bobbed his head faster and sucked harder. Kyle arched his back and groaned as shockwaves of pleasure rippled through his body, leaving a trail of fire behind. For a blissful moment, his mind became empty, a blank canvas drawn in by the afterglow of sex. It had all happened too fast but he couldn't have slowed it down even if his life had depended upon it. He'd been too charged up for far too long.

"Did you like it?" Logan asked, a moment later, as he licked the last drop of Kyle's seed.

"That was the best thing that has happened to me in a very, very long time," he said, grinning from ear to ear. "Sorry about finishing so fast."

By now Logan was standing and holding Kyle by his waist. "Don't be silly."

"But you didn't come."

Logan chuckled. "You know, sex doesn't always have to involve two people orgasming. I loved doing this for you."

Kyle smiled and hugged Logan, suddenly realizing his jeans were around his ankles. He ignored them and kept hugging Logan, his lover's musky scent filling his nostrils. Logan's cock throbbed against him and Kyle felt a sparkle of lust coming alive, albeit a timid one.

Kyle leaned back. "I know you liked what we just did but I'm sensing you need something more," and he grabbed Logan's cock over his jeans.

Logan gasped and blushed, his pupils dilating as he looked straight at Kyle. "I'd say you're right. But are you ready to go at it again?"

Kyle looked down and his dick twitched. "Give it a couple more minutes."

Logan laughed and kissed Kyle, grabbing him tightly. "How about we take this upstairs?" he said, wiggling his eyebrows.

***

Kyle was on the bed, lying on his back, partly covered by the sheets, half-asleep and feeling as though he was hovering above himself. As he drifted in and out of sleep, he thought on how he was happier than ever, still having a hard time believing this was really happening to him. The fire Logan had started inside him had been rekindled as soon as they'd stepped into his bedroom. They were both naked a moment later, grinding on the bed, Kyle grabbing both their throbbing cocks, drunk on desire. Feeling Logan's weight on him was wonderful and there were no words to describe how good it felt when he finally came all over him. It had been exhausting and Kyle was left thirsty and famished. Logan had gone downstairs to prepare them a snack after a quick shower together, but Kyle was now more sleepy than hungry.

He was practically asleep when a scream downstairs jolted him awake and his whole body snapped upright with a jerk. What was that? He wasn't entirely sure what he'd heard but a second screech told him he wasn't dreaming. What in the hell?

Kyle jumped out of bed and ran downstairs, his heart beating like crazy, dread filling his veins, fearing something bad had happened to Logan. He jumped two steps at a time until he landed on the ground floor. His eyes scanned the room but his brain took a second to understand the drama unfolding before him. As soon as reality kicked in, though, he felt his blood fleeing him. Jessica was pointing something like a canister at Logan, who'd covered his eyes in pain, one hand reaching to her in a gesture of truce.

"Jessica!" Kyle yelped. "What are you doing?"

Jessica turned to him and her jaw fell. She glared at him, scanning him from head to toe, a shocked expression on her face, and Kyle remembered he was buck naked. Jessica's expression went from shocked to angry.

"What's the meaning of this?" she demanded, her finger waving around the room in an accusatory tone.

Kyle covered himself with his hands. He opened and closed his mouth a couple of times, but he'd no excuse that would make the situation any better.

"What are you doing here? And what have you done to Logan?" Kyle said, hurrying to Logan's side. Although he was still trying to cover himself up, Kyle realized there was nothing there she hadn't seen before. Logan seemed in pain and kept rubbing his eyes.

Jessica huffed. "He came out of nowhere and I maced him. I thought he was going to attack me or something." She scoffed, scanning Logan who was still in too much pain to care as he stumbled about the room, his penis dangling.

"Stay here," Kyle said to her as he grabbed Logan by his shoulders. "I'm gonna help him wash his eyes."

Kyle helped Logan to the downstairs' bathroom and pointed him at the sink.

"Are you okay? I'm so sorry about this. I had no idea she'd appear without warning and use her key. She never told me she was coming, just said she'd think about it."

"It's okay. Go talk to her," Logan groaned, while washing his eyes and face with copious amounts of water.

Kyle now realized Jessica had seen them both together, stark naked. The reality of it sank in and he panicked, seeing her use it all as a weapon against him in getting sole custody of Ryan.

"You think you're gonna be okay if I leave you here?" he said to Logan.

Logan mumbled he was fine while continuing to splash generous amounts of water onto his eyes. Grabbing a spare towel and wrapping it around his waist, Kyle went to face Jessica. She was pacing the living room, livid, her nostrils flaring. She turned to him when she heard his footsteps.

"So this is how you plan to raise our child from now on? And here I was, thinking of giving you a chance, of coming to see the real you. Well, let me tell you: I've seen it and I don't like it a bit!" Jessica had worked herself up, her face now flushed. She seemed angrier than ever.

"We're both adults here, Jessica, and we both know sex is a part of life. I'm not gonna apologize for having a life. You should've warned me you were coming."

Jessica stopped in her tracks and squinted at Kyle. "You said I should come! You should have been the one to warn me you'd be flaunting around your newfound sexuality. You didn't waste any time turning fully gay, now did you? You're disgusting, Kyle, you really are."

Kyle felt something inside him snap. "Shut up, Jessica, okay? Just shut up! I've tried to be the bigger person here and do right by you because I felt you didn't deserve what I did to you. But you've been nothing but a bitch to me ever since I had the courage to be honest with the both of us. I get it, okay? I get that you're angry, but what were you expecting me to do? Huh? You'd rather have me keep lying to you? Maybe even cheat on you with a guy? Is that it?"

The silence that came between them was pierced only by Kyle's quick breathing. He watched as Jessica's demeanor changed into cold anger and he realized he'd gone too far in calling her a bitch. And he hadn't meant it. It had just been his anger.

"I'm the bitch?" Jessica at last managed to get out, her voice loud and shrill. "Fuck you, Kyle. I'd rather be a bitch than a lying bastard who uses people to get by because he's too much of a coward to be honest!"

Kyle felt sick to his stomach. Deep down he knew Jessica was right. She was right, and there was nothing he could say that would change it.

Jessica was breathing fast and trembling, pale as a sheet. Kyle set his hands on his hips and sighed. "I'm sorry, Jess. I didn't mean to call you a bitch. I don't want to fight with you. This is hard enough as it is. I… I'm sorry things turned out this way."

A lone tear slid down Jessica's face and onto her pursed lips. "You chose this path, Kyle, not me." She strode past him, looking straight ahead as she approached the front door.

"Wait. Jess, wait!"

She stopped just before the door and turned to him. Her eyes were red, the lone tear now no longer alone. "What?"

"It's too late to return to the city. Please, stay."

Her lip trembled as she opened her mouth to speak. "I... I can't. I'll get a room in the city. We'll talk tomorrow."

Jessica went out and closed the door behind her. Kyle sighed. He felt terrible. Jessica had no right in coming here without telling him, but he had to admit he hadn't handled the situation at all well. He regretted his angry outburst, especially because there was definitely something off with Jessica, as if she were hiding her suffering behind that angry mask. He needed to make things right. She didn't deserve the way he'd spoken to her. And nor could he stand the thought of losing Ryan.

Chapter Twenty

Logan was walking Buddy in Greenville's central park, a leafy area with big, imposing trees that provided a welcome haven from the sun's heat. One could walk from end to end in only ten minutes, but it was, nevertheless, his favorite part of town because it was so like the big, green expanse he had around his own house. And the park helped him pretend he wasn't surrounded by buildings, streets and cars. It shielded him from modern life's noises. According to his work colleagues, the mayor had remodeled the park a few years before with a pond deep enough to harbor different kinds of fish and a small community of ducks and swans. It was all very peaceful and idyllic, although Buddy always felt inclined to run after the birds. It was embarrassing to have one's dog disturbing everyone, so Logan scolded Buddy until he learned he mustn't bark or chase after the ducks.

He checked his phone for the millionth time that morning and put it back in his pocket. Kyle was supposed to call and meet him here but there was still no word from him. Kyle had gone after Jessica, to try and have a civilized talk with her about the previous night, and also about their future. Logan winced. The previous night. What a disastrous way to meet Kyle's soon-to-be ex-wife. Between being startled by her and maced, it had been a real mess. He'd never been hit by pepper spray, not even when he used to break into rich people's mansions. And he hoped he never would again. The night had been perfect up until that. Being able to be there for Kyle's first time with a man had made him happier than anything, but he was now worried that their timing had been awful and the previous night would weigh heavily against Kyle in his fight for Ryan's custody.

Buddy started to bark again and pulled at the leash, bringing Logan back from his musings.

"Stop that, Buddy. I told you the ducks are off-limits."

Buddy kept woofing, though, and Logan heard a woman yelling. He looked ahead and saw a kid waving from within the pond, clearly shouting for help, fighting to keep his head above water. Logan didn't think twice. He let go of Buddy's leash and sprang forward, running at full pelt. The child looked like he was losing strength and didn't have much more time. Logan willed himself into running faster and soon dove headfirst into the pond. The kid was now underwater but Logan reached him in a couple of powerful strokes. Grabbing him around his chest, Logan kicked his legs out as strongly as he could, pushing them both to the surface.

Logan gasped for air as he emerged, then made sure the little boy's head was above the water and swam ashore with him. A woman was crying and screaming "My baby" when Logan dragged them both onto solid ground. A small crowd had gathered, but he ignored them. The kid wasn't breathing and needed CPR, and fast.

"Someone call 911!" he pleaded. Ignoring the woman wailing next to him, he tilted the boy's head back, found the right location on his chest with one hand and then covered it with the other, doing a quick series of compressions. He lifted the kid's chin, opened his airways and covered his mouth with his own, while pinching the boy's nose. Logan gave him two short breaths and the kid began to cough and spat some water. Logan leaned back and let himself breathe.

"My baby!" the woman wailed, now in floods of tears as she embraced the child who seemed to be coming to his senses.

Logan hadn't had time to see who the woman was, not until she snatched the boy from his arms. Her disheveled hair covered part of her face while she rocked the child back and forth. But even though her face was contorted in pain and ran with mascara, there was something familiar about her. Logan leaned in and squinted, trying to get a better look. She glanced up and Logan's stomach churned. It was the same woman who had screamed at him and Kyle by the lake. He tensed, fearing more insults were on her lips as she parted them to speak.

"Thank you," she sobbed. "Thank you for saving my grandson."

Her words took a moment to penetrate the defensive wall he'd quickly put up around himself, expecting the worse. But in her eyes there was nothing but gratitude. Logan sensed it, smiled and nodded. Words were meaningless in a moment like this. He worried that the fragile bridge they'd built in that instant might come crashing down at any moment. Around them, people began applauding. Logan heard someone say "Hero" and felt uncomfortable in all the attention.

A bark and a wet lick made him realize he'd forgotten about Buddy. He rubbed the dog's back and got up, smiling embarrassedly at all the people around him as he tried to slip away, Buddy trotting at his heels. The impromptu swim had at least cooled him down, but he would have to go and change. There was green slime on his T-shirt and he smelled like a fish tank that hadn't been cleaned in months.

"Shit! My phone," he said under his breath. In the hurry to help the boy, he'd completely forgotten about it. Logan sighed as he fished it out of his chino shorts' pocket. He flipped it open but it was dead. Drenched and dead. Shit. How was he supposed to talk to Kyle now? He'd have to buy a new one. Logan sighed. He wasn't exactly swimming in money. That had been the reason he'd bought a flip phone to begin with, the cheapest he'd found in the store. The assistant had given him a strange look when he'd declined to buy a smartphone and went for a feature one instead, like he was some kind of alien with no clue about what people were supposed to buy these days.

Logan looked at the phone as he turned it around in his hand, hoping he could somehow bring it back to life. Maybe if

133

he took the battery out and put it to dry for a couple of days it would then work again, but he knew it was just wishful thinking. He put the phone back in his pocket and grabbed his wallet. It was also dripping, but fortunately the few bucks and cards he had in there would dry out without a problem. He rubbed his forehead after putting his wallet away. He needed to find a payphone and tell Kyle what had happened. He should have been calling any minute and Logan was worried about his meeting with Jessica.

Unfortunately, and although he had stared at Kyle's number so many times in the past few weeks, his mind was a dark canvas when he tried to recall it.

"Well, we're screwed, Buddy," he said, staring at his faithful friend.

Logan was torn between staying there soaking wet and unreachable, hoping Kyle would show up and they'd somehow find each other, and going to the hotel where he was meeting Jessica, to wait for him there.

"Maybe there's no harm in going there. I'll be in and out real quick, right?"

Buddy lifted his ears, watching Logan, his tail wagging. He replied with a woof, as if telling him it was a bad idea.

Logan frowned. "I don't care if you think it is. There's nothing else I can do," and he began walking towards the small hotel. "He's supposed to call me and now I don't have a phone."

Buddy said nothing while walking by his side, his tongue lolling from his mouth. But there was a disapproving look in his eyes. Or maybe it was all in Logan's head. After all, Buddy would have no idea what he was talking about, anyway.

***

Logan stared at the Blue Willow hotel entrance, wondering if he should wait outside instead of going in. But it was too hot even to consider it, enduring the scorching sun pure madness, even for a couple of minutes. It was so hot his clothes had almost dried out during the short walk from the park. At least the problem of his soaking wet clothes had almost been solved. Now, all he needed to do was get rid of the fishy smell that was getting worse by the minute.

He went inside, straight into the all-enveloping coolness of air conditioning. He sighed, relieved, and scanned the place. Right in front of him, down the small lobby, was a counter behind which a couple of employees were taking calls. On the left side were the elevators and to the right what seemed to be a bar or a restaurant. Logan stood there, thinking that maybe the hotel staff wouldn't like the idea of him walking in here with his dog. Maybe he could leave Kyle a message saying there had been a change of plans and he'd gone home. He was about to walk to the counter to find out when the elevator dinged. The doors opened and Jessica walked out, a diaphanous wave of gossamer fabric behind her. With that summer dress, there was no question she was prepared to face the heat outside, and Logan watched her with a fresh pair of eyes. He hadn't managed to get a good look at her the previous night, not with his eyes full of pepper spray, but now he could see why Kyle had fallen for her. Her heart-shaped face was home to expressive, round brown eyes and pink, plump lips that gave her a girlish, cute look. Waves of cascading hair framed her face beautifully and made her look like one of those shampoo models. In that microsecond before she recognized him, Logan saw how frail and delicate she seemed and he softened towards her. The subtle aggravation he'd been feeling towards her since she'd attacked him now evaporated in an instant.

Jessica stopped and they both stared at each other, as if paralyzed. Logan blinked, worried he'd make things even worse for Kyle. Where was he, anyway? If she was in the lobby, then Kyle must have been here too, so he had to have missed him. Jessica's shocked expression evaporated as she carried on towards Logan and the exit behind him. She stopped in front of him, though, and gave him a fixed look.

But her expression appeared to soften when she noticed Buddy.

"If you're looking for Kyle, he already left," she said.

Logan tried to persuade his pursed lips to stretch into a smile. "My phone died and I was going to leave him a message."

Jessica sighed, her shoulders dropping. "Can I offer you a drink, then?"

Logan jaw almost hit the floor but he composed himself before looking like a surprised fool. He looked at Jessica. She seemed somehow defeated, like everything was too much for her to bear any more. Although it probably wasn't the best idea, he nodded and they walked through into the hotel's bar. He felt curious about her. And maybe talking to Jessica over a drink would be a good way of helping Kyle.

"Sir, I'm sorry, but you can't come in here with your dog," the bartender said when they walked in. He was a slightly overweight man, probably in his thirties, but somehow seemed older.

"It's just for five minutes. It's too hot outside," Logan pleaded. "He's really well behaved and I promise you he won't disturb anyone."

The bartender wrinkled his nose. "Okay, but if he starts barking you'll have to leave."

Logan thanked him and turned to Jessica, noting how she seemed to be closely observing the situation. She looked away as soon as their eyes met.

"Can I have a tonic water with a slice of lemon, please?" she said as they both sat on the bar stools.

Logan asked for the same. It was too early to start drinking beer, and anyway, he didn't want to give her the wrong impression. They both waited in silence for their drinks. When the bartender returned, Jessica glanced at Logan. "This is awkward. Maybe I shouldn't have invited my husband's lover to have a drink with me."

Logan cringed. She was right, though. What was he thinking? "I'm sorry for what happened last night but don't punish Kyle for it."

Jessica turned to him, frowning. "Is that what you think? That I'm out to punish Kyle for what he did to me?" She scoffed then drank from her water. "Of course the only woman in this love triangle would be made out to be the bad guy. What has that jerk told you? That I'm trying to stop him from seeing his son?"

"Kyle mentioned something about—"

"He spent his life lying to me about who he was. Why should I trust him with my child? How can I believe he'll do the right thing and be a decent person from now on? Because, let me tell you, he's been a real jerk for the past couple of years, and that has nothing to do with his sexual orientation."

Jessica spoke without looking directly at Logan, as if she didn't want to acknowledge he was really there.

"I don't think you mean that."

"And what the hell do you know about me?" Jessica rubbed her forehead. "Marrying Kyle was one of the happiest days of my life. He was everything I'd ever wanted in a man: loving and kind and smart. I felt the luckiest girl alive when he noticed me instead of all the other girls he always had chasing after him. He made me feel special and loved, and then it all changed without so much as a warning. He betrayed me. He betrayed us!"

Logan sighed. "In the past few weeks I've had the opportunity to get to know Kyle, and to see he's a wonderful guy. He feels guilty for what he's done to you and for having made you suffer. I know it's not my place to say this, but he didn't deceive you on purpose. Sometimes being honest with ourselves is one of the hardest things we can do, and I guess Kyle spent a lot of time lying to himself. I know he doesn't love you as you probably wanted him to, but I also know that he cares about you very much."

Jessica sucked her teeth for a while, then said, "You're right. It's not your place to say anything." She drank from her water again and they both stayed silent for a moment. Then she added: "But I appreciate your honesty." She turned to him and her eyes drifted to Buddy. "I'm sorry. I'm trying to hate you for something that's not really your fault. You seem like a decent person. Well, at least you're good to your dog." A timid smile danced across her lips but was quickly followed by a sadness that engulfed it before it had had any chance to blossom.

"I'm not even gonna pretend I know how you feel. I've had my fair share of disappointment and I can truly say to you that this is not the end. It may seem like it, but it's not."

They kept silent for another moment, each nursing their beverages and entertaining their own thoughts.

"I'm sorry for having attacked you yesterday. But you scared me to death. I promise I didn't do it because you're...with Kyle." Jessica's voice had quivered.

"I understand. You were caught by surprise."

"I just came here because he insisted, and I suppose I felt bad for not giving him a chance. I feel like he's a whole different person, that I don't know the real him, not anymore." Jessica placed her head between her hands. "Why am I talking to you, anyway?"

"I'm sorry things didn't work out for you."

She sniffed. "So am I."

Logan kept staring at her, not knowing what more to say. He felt Jessica was a good person who had probably only acted the way she had out of being so hurt. It was clear she loved Kyle, but it was also clear she didn't know how to deal with all of this.

"I know this is going to sound weird, but would you like to have dinner with me and Kyle?" Jessica lifted her head from her hands and turned to Logan, confusion on her face. "You said you wanted to know the real him," Logan said when she didn't say anything. "This could be a first step. I could pick you up here. Or Kyle could pick you up. Whichever you prefer."

After a few moments of her gaze darting about his face, Jessica finally shrugged and said, "Sure, why not? Can't be worse than last night, right?"

Chapter Twenty-One

As soon as Logan arrived home, he went into the bathroom, stripped off his smelly clothes and took a long shower, scrubbing his skin hard. After having spent the morning smelling like fish, it felt really good finally to be able to get rid of it. He was already going downstairs, all fresh and feeling lighter, when he heard Buddy barking. A moment later, Kyle came in.

"What's all this about the dinner Jessica says you invited her for?"

Logan smiled. "She told you about my dead phone?"

Kyle closed the door behind him and petted Buddy. "Yeah, she told me. She also told me you reeked of fish. What happened?"

Logan approached Kyle, kissed him and told him all about his morning adventure, how he'd saved the kid from drowning at the park and had met Jessica at the hotel.

"So you not only saved the kid, but he was the grandson of that awful woman? This really is a small town." By now they were in the living room, comfortably sitting on the couch.

"Can you believe it? But I don't know about 'Awful'. She seemed pretty humbled."

"Of course she did. You had just saved her grandson. At least now we know she's not completely heartless." Kyle raised his eyebrows, his gaze unfocused. "Man, talk about coincidences." He focused his eyes on Logan again. "But that doesn't explain why you felt the need to invite Jessica over."

"We had a talk and we kind of connected in some way. I don't know if that makes any sense, but we did. I also felt sorry for her. She seemed so frail. She said she came here hoping to know the real you. Instead, she saw me naked."

Kyle sighed. "If I weren't so worried, I'd be saying something along the lines of how lucky she was." Kyle's smile dimmed. "I just hope this won't backfire."

"Why would it?"

"I keep thinking if it were me in her shoes, and I'm worried she might change her mind about all this. She seems a bit unhinged. I don't know. Maybe it's all in my head."

"Maybe it is. She didn't seem to be the vindictive type. Granted, she's hurt, but I mainly think she's just really sad and trying to cope with it all. Didn't you say she seemed willing to compromise when you guys met at her place a couple of weeks ago? And remember, she even came here as you asked."

"Yeah, but that was before…well, catching us buck naked. I don't know what to think anymore."

"How about we take this one step at a time and assume she's being honest? I don't think she's out to get you. Unless she's a great actress and I've been completely fooled."

Kyle turned to Logan. "Dinner, ugh?"

"Yep."

"Here, in your house?"

"Yep."

Kyle sighed. "You cook and I'll drive her here."

"Deal."

***

As the time for the dinner approached, Logan began to feel nervous. Having Jessica over had seemed a good idea at first. Earlier, in the bar, she'd seemed frail, suffering for a husband who didn't love her back. That had made Logan's heart ache. He just wanted to do something nice for her, take care of her, stroke her hair and tell her everything would be fine despite knowing this didn't make sense for at least a couple of reasons: on the one hand she was a grown woman who seemed to know how to take care of herself. On the other...well, he was currently sleeping with her soon-to-be ex-husband, which would certainly not help their relationship.

Logan tried to cast his worries away as he carried a big bowl of salad from the kitchen to the living room. Buddy appeared to sense his nervousness and kept running around, barking from time to time, almost tripping him before he could place the bowl on the table, but he didn't have the heart to scold him.

He finally placed the salad safely on the table and covered it with a paper napkin. Dinner would be light as that day's heat was asking for something that didn't involve too much cooking. He'd decided to prepare a salad with arugula, smoked salmon and feta cheese. It was ready and waiting for Jessica to arrive, seasoned with the dry ingredients for now. The wet ones would be mixed in only after she arrived, otherwise the whole thing would morph into a mushy mess in a couple of minutes.

Logan scanned the living room. The table was set, the food ready and there was nothing left to do. He went back to the kitchen just to check the time on the wall clock. There was nothing else to do but wait and control that unexpected and growing anxiety he hadn't accounted for.

"Wanna go wait for Kyle in the backyard? Hmm?"

Buddy looked up at him and woofed. Before they could go out, though, the doorbell rang and Buddy ran to the door, barking happily.

"Well, I guess we'll have to postpone it, then," Logan said to himself, watching Buddy excitedly wagging his tail and staring up at the door.

Logan went to open it, trying not to make a big deal out of the night. He would be charming, Jessica would realize Kyle didn't mean any harm and they'd find a way to make things work.

He found an awkward Kyle on the porch, Jessica by his side. Buddy ran out and began jumping between the two. Jessica seemed hesitant before Buddy's excitement.

"Buddy, come here," Logan snapped, and Buddy complied, his ears slightly down but still wagging his tail. Logan focused his attention on his guests again. "Hi. Please, come in. And don't worry, he's harmless."

Kyle and Jessica came in, a watchful Buddy sitting by Logan's side.

"He seems such a good boy," Jessica said, crouching and reaching her hand to him so he could sniff it. Buddy obliged and proceeded to lick her.

Logan closed the door behind them and exchanged a surprised look with Kyle. Buddy had seen her back in the hotel, but it wasn't like him to be all friendly like that with a stranger. Maybe it meant she wasn't that bad.

"I don't think I've ever seen anyone win over Buddy's heart this fast," Logan said, trying to make small talk.

"Jess has always had a way with dogs," Kyle said.

Jessica stood up, a mildly embarrassed smile on her lips.

"And it shows." There was a small silence, during which they all looked at each other. "What can I get you to drink?" Logan finally said to Jessica.

The night went by without a hiccup. Jessica loved Logan's salad and praised the house and the surrounding area as lovely and peaceful, the exact opposite, she told him, of her apartment in the city where the street noise always managed to seep in, despite it having double-glazed windows. Nevertheless, Logan felt as though he was in some kind of formal event where Jessica was one of those guests you had to treat with the utmost deference. Their chat was friendly but had a plastic sheen to it that he couldn't shake off. It was clear she was making a great effort to be amicable and polite, but the sadness Logan had seen in the hotel was still there, looming in her eyes, overflowing into her delicate features. If she was here to know more about the real Kyle, then this polite chit-chat wouldn't help. Still, Logan was unsure if he should meddle and throw something real into the conversation or just let the small talk flow. Maybe she wasn't ready for it yet. Maybe the only thing they could both bear right now was talking about nothing.

"...and the room is finished. You have to see it. It's really nice. Logan is really skilled and the furniture is even better than our...than the one in your apartment."

Logan tuned into the chit-chat again, listening to Kyle trip over his own words. She looked from him to Logan.

"So you're a carpenter?"

Logan nodded. "I am. I work in a local company that specializes in custom furniture."

Jessica placed her fork on her plate and turned to Kyle, her eyes narrowing. "That's how you two met?"

There it was: chit-chat over.

Kyle glanced at Logan before saying, "Yes. I met Logan when I went to the store he works in to check their furniture."

Jessica frowned, as if placing some pieces together. "That was, what, two months ago?"

"Something like that, yes," Kyle said.

Jessica scoffed and a hurt smiled bloomed on her face. "Now that's what I'd call great home service."

"Jess, please. It wasn't like that."

"Like what, Kyle? Hmm? Because from where I'm sitting it looks like you jumped into the pants of another man as soon as you got here." Her fair complexion was now rosy. She scoffed again. "Unless you two were already acquainted. Is that it? Did you know him before deciding to end things with me?"

Kyle leaned back at the accusing finger Jessica now pointed at him. "What? That's insane. I didn't know Logan back then."

"You don't have to lie to me. Not anymore."

"I'm not lying!"

Jessica narrowed her eyes. "Oh, that's rich. I honestly don't know what's worse, Kyle: you fucking some guy on the side while we were still together or going with the first one you meet after dumping me!"

Kyle tensed up. "Not that this is any of your concern, but Logan's not some guy. I'm not some slut who goes around fucking complete strangers."

The silence that then filled the room was almost palpable. Logan was torn between staying invisible and saying something that didn't sound confrontational. He ended up staying quiet. He wanted to help but feared whatever it was Jessica heard from him right now would probably make matters worse.

Kyle ran his fingers through his hair, tousling it. "I'm sorry I'm not the husband you wanted or deserved, Jess. But it's not fair to portray me like I'm heartless. I'm not."

Jessica sat with her arms crossed over her chest. The anger that had only a moment before flared up all over her face now became a sadness that made her seem small. She stared at the wall and quietly wept. The night had clearly derailed into some kind of weird purgatory and Logan's idea of having a pleasant evening during which Jessica could see the real Kyle had long gone out of the window. Buddy came out of nowhere, his claws clicking on the wooden floor as he approached Jessica. He sat by her side and looked up at her, his big dark eyes beseeching, then placed a paw on her leg, startling her. She looked down at him and he whined softly before getting up and propping his head on her lap.

"Buddy! Come here." Logan called softly.

Buddy complied, but Jessica only watched him walk away from her before wiping the tears from her face and getting to her feet.

"I need to get some fresh air. I can't do this," she said, looking askance at Kyle, as if unable to meet his eyes.

"I'll drive you back to town, then," Kyle said, standing up.

"You don't have to. I'll get a cab."

"We don't have any around here," Logan said.

"I'll drive you back," Kyle insisted.

Jessica nodded in silence. "Thank you for dinner," she said to Logan in a small voice, and then they were gone.

Logan watched them get into Kyle's SUV, his gaze following its taillights until it vanished into the night. Somehow, he felt guilty for it being him who was with Kyle, for making Jessica suffer. He knew this was nonsense of course, as Kyle had already left her before they had met, but none of this mess was fair to anyone, and especially not to her. The love of her life had been yanked away from her, yet she was trying to be understanding and listen to what Kyle had to say. Logan sighed. Strangely enough his heart was with Jessica.

Chapter Twenty-Two

The silence of the night amplified every sound inside the car: the tires pressing on a million pebbles while rolling over the dirt road; the creaking of the plastic console behind the steering wheel; Jessica's breathing. As Kyle drove to town he tried to come up with something to say, something that would break the ice and make that bad blood between them go away. But he didn't know what to say. He didn't know how to convey to her how deeply sorry he was for everything, but especially for not having had the courage to be himself sooner and so spare them all the suffering.

"There's a lot I regret, but I don't regret the time we've had together," he said. "You're absolutely right when you say I'm a coward. I am. I know I should've been myself when, back in high school, Wayne dared me to kiss and grope some random girl to prove I wasn't gay. He'd caught me looking at him in the locker room and so I did what he told me to do. I know I shouldn't have gone to second base with Amy in senior year just because that's what guys were supposed to do, and I was too afraid of what would happen if I let myself think for one second on what I really felt. And I know I shouldn't have married you. I know that. But I don't regret it, not one bit. It brought me Ryan and I love him more than anything, more that I can express in words. I'm sorry for deceiving you, Jess. I really am."

Kyle stole a peek at Jessica. She was gazing at the stars, elbow resting on the open window, a hand on her skirt. She stayed silent for what seemed like an eternity, but then said, "You know, when we exchanged vows I never imagined that one day I'd be meeting your boyfriend. There was a lot going through my mind that day. I was afraid my cousin Barry would get drunk and ruin everything, or that our mothers would engage in another heated argument, but not in a million years did I imagine having to deal with your boyfriend." She turned to face him. "You know what I was afraid of that day? That I'd grow old and wrinkly and you'd trade me in for someone younger; that you'd realize we had nothing in common and stop loving me. I was so scared of losing you, Kyle. Up until we met I really thought that all of my dreams of meeting a decent guy were just that: dreams. And then you came along. You were so different, so sensitive and caring, always putting me ahead of your needs, always going the extra mile to make me happy. I should've known no guy is that caring."

They stayed silent for a moment, Kyle focusing on the winding road. "In a way, I guess I was trying to make up for the fact that deep down I knew that you knew? I was in a deep state of denial, Jess, but I never meant to hurt you." Kyle stole a peek at her but couldn't really see her face. The dashboard glow was too faint to light anything but the contour of Jessica's face.

The song of the million cicadas outside grew and filled the silence between them. Kyle felt like the bond that had once existed between them was now irreparably broken, and he felt sorry for them both.

"Remember that time I left the house in the middle of the night because you were craving ice cream? I think you were seven months pregnant. That summer night was so hot our apartment was actually hotter than outside. You were miserable, sweating and nauseated, and the ice cream was the only thing that didn't make you sick, remember?" Kyle paused to give her some time to acknowledge the memory, but Jessica stayed silent. "I had had no sleep for two days and was practically delirious, but even so I went searching for a place to buy you ice cream. I was trying to show I was in it with you, and if you couldn't sleep, neither would I. I loved you so much in that moment, Jess. I loved you although you were cranky and yelling. I was responsible for your state." Kyle chuckled as a tear slid down his face. "Knowing that you were carrying my child made me love you more than I'd ever loved anyone before. And I wanted to show you that, wanted you to know I'd do anything for you. And so I went searching for ice cream and said nothing about the feelings I had swirling around inside, feelings that made me question myself. I said nothing because I loved you and wanted us to be a family, I wanted us to be happy. I loved you Jess, but I couldn't love you enough to make myself straight. I wanted to make this work, Jess. I really did. Now I want to do whatever it takes to show you that this is the only option I had, that I didn't destroy our marriage on a whim. I had to do this, Jess. Lying about who I was to myself was consuming me, making me an ugly person. I didn't want that for you or for Ryan."

Kyle stopped the car. They were in front of Jessica's hotel. He cleaned the tears off his face and turned to her. She was looking at her hands, playing with her fingers, her watery eyes dripping all over her skirt.

Jessica lifted her chin and locked eyes with him. "I want to believe you, I really do, but tonight I can't. I just can't."

Kyle breathed raggedly. "Can we at least talk tomorrow?"

A lone car passed by on the deserted street. Somehow the noise from its engine seemed louder and more aggressive than it should.

"I need some time to think about everything you've said, what I want for me, for our son… I'm just overwhelmed right now and can't think straight. I'll call you."

Kyle watched Jessica leave the car and go into the hotel. He'd poured his heart out and had been honest with her. Now he just hoped he'd managed to get through to her somehow, because he felt like he'd lost Jessica already. He couldn't afford to lose his son, too.

Chapter Twenty-Three

Logan left work feeling tired. The day had been a long one but he still wanted to go buy some groceries before returning home. He wanted to treat Kyle to a comforting meal and maybe help him forget for a couple of hours about his feud with Jessica. Ever since that disaster of a dinner a couple of days before, Kyle had been quieter, more contemplative. Logan feared he was having second thoughts about his decision to leave Jessica, or worse, about their relationship, but had said nothing. He didn't want to sound selfish when Kyle was clearly going through such a lot. Logan ended up rationalizing that he was inferring too much from Kyle's moodiness. He was probably just worried about his son.

"Excuse me."

Logan had been about to go into the store when he heard the voice. He turned around and saw the woman from the lake. His heart started beating faster, as if expecting her to pounce on him. He breathed in and loosened his tensed muscles. He'd been so deep in his thoughts while walking that he hadn't noticed her. Now she was looking at him as if waiting to be acknowledged, her hands clutched together below her waistline.

"Can I help you?" Logan asked.

She scanned him from head to toe and tried to smile. "I wasn't able to thank you properly the other day," she said, tentatively. "For helping my grandson."

"There's no need for that. I only did what anyone would do."

"Even so, you were the only one who stepped forward. So, thank you. I'm sure it wasn't easy for you after… Well, after our last encounter."

Logan frowned for a moment, trying to understand what she meant. "You mean that day at the lake?"

"Well, yes. You people tend to be proud but I'm happy you managed to put that past you."

Logan was taken aback. "People like me? What do you mean 'Like me'? I didn't save your grandson to prove something to you, or to anyone else. I did it because the child was in danger and it was the right thing to do. Stop making assumptions about what you think people like me are supposed to behave like, and maybe invest some time in tearing down those bigoted ideas you have."

The woman opened and closed her mouth several times and grabbed the sides of her cardigan, closing it even more, as if trying to protect herself from Logan's words. "I'm not trying to antagonize you. I'm just not used to…well, dealing with people like yourself," she said, apologetically.

Logan sighed. What at first had seemed a cheap shot at him was now beginning to look like a lack of tact. Whatever the case, though, Logan was having a hard time deciding how to respond. But then he thought about the chasm that existed between his real self and the notion people had about him, the ex-convict, and decided to cut her some slack.

"As I said, you don't have to thank me. I just did what anyone would do. Have a nice day, ma'am." Logan tried to smile and prepared to leave.

"Please, wait," she said when Logan was already heading to the store. He looked over his shoulder and saw the woman's face marred by an expression of suffering while she intertwined her fingers feverishly. She continued: "Do you think my husband… Do you think he's gay?"

The woman had almost whispered the last part. Logan froze, trying to decide if he'd heard her correctly. Did she really ask him if her husband was gay?

"I'm sorry but I'm not sure I'm following you," he said, turning back and approaching her.

The woman seemed nervous. She looked around, as if expecting to find someone listening to them. Then she grabbed Logan by his arm and pulled him closer. "Can I buy you a cup of coffee?"

Now that was unexpected. "I can't. I have to be somewhere."

Her shoulders dropped and she sighed. "I think my husband might be gay and I thought you could...well, help me figure out if I'm right."

"And why do you think I'd be able to help?"

It was obvious this subject was making her uncomfortable. After a moment's silence, she finally said, "He never really showed any interest in being with me... You know, in the bedroom. And as you yourself are a...homosexual, I thought that maybe ... that maybe you could tell me if I'm right or not."

Logan raised his eyebrows. That was information he never expected to be discussing with a total stranger, much less a woman like her. He wondered if this was the reason she seemed so obsessed with depriving gays of their basic rights.

"I'm not sure I'd be able to help."

"I just want you to be honest with me and tell me if you think my husband is gay." She kept twisting the ring on her finger while staring at him with attentive eyes, like he held the key to her happiness.

"I'm sorry, but I really can't tell you that. Being gay is not something you wear on your forehead. It's not that linear. I think you should talk to your husband about what's bothering you. Ask him to be honest with you."

The woman seemed disappointed. "Thank you."

"You're welcome."

"And please, don't mention this to anyone."

Her pleading tone made Logan look at her with different eyes. She seemed a sad, frightened woman now, battling her inner demons like everyone else. Logan promised not to talk to anyone else about their conversation and went inside the grocery store, thinking about how bizarre the afternoon had turned out to be.

***

"Have you heard from her?" Logan asked as he turned off the stove. Kyle had arrived a moment before and still had that look of sadness about him, the one he'd sported since their dinner with Jessica.

"No. She hasn't called and it's driving me insane. Today, I found myself picking up the phone every half hour, trying to decide if it's too early to call her myself. I don't know if I should wait or if I should call. I feel that if I call I might end up making matters worse, but this uncertainty is killing me."

Logan approached the stool Kyle was sitting on and hugged him. "She'll come around. You'll see."

"I hope you're right," Kyle said, looking up at Logan.

"I have a story that will take your mind off things. Wanna hear?"

"Sure."

Logan went back to the stove and began serving the food. They'd be dining homemade burgers accompanied by a green salad. "You won't believe who approached me just before coming home. Remember that crazy lady from the lake? She wanted me to help her find out if her husband's gay. Can you believe it?"

"What?"

Logan told him about his awkward conversation and Kyle couldn't believe what he was hearing. Logan finished by saying, "I bet you that's why she was collecting those signatures the other day, trying to stop gay marriage."

"You're probably right. I mean, it makes a lot of sense that her distaste for gays is just an escape valve for her real problems—her suspicions about her husband. Maybe those more vocal about it are just closeted gays, mad about the ones who had the courage to come out, you know?"

Logan smiled. "That's an interesting observation. Were you violent towards gays before coming out?"

Kyle thought for a moment. "Not violent, no." He looked at the floor. "But I've said things I'm not proud of. I was really stupid. I was trying to be one of the guys and avoid the spotlight, so I said and did some things I regret."

"Maybe you're right," Logan said. "In her case, she is secretly mad at her husband for not desiring her like she wanted him to."

Logan placed the plates on the kitchen table. Kyle's face was still shadowed by sorrow. Logan's story clearly hadn't helped.

"Are you having second thoughts about this? About having come out?" Logan knew he was being selfish but he had to ask. He had to know if the thought of losing his son was making Kyle doubt what he wanted for his life. After all, it was more than understandable if Kyle chose his son over him.

Kyle looked up at Logan, confusion filling his eyes. "Do you think I'm having doubts about us?"

Logan sat next to him. "I think you may be wondering if coming out was worth it, yes."

"I'm not. I mean, I'm not gonna lie. This fight with Jessica over Ryan has been hard, but I'm not questioning what I did. I told you, it was making me an angry and frustrated person. I don't want that for my son."

"You've been so sad the last couple of days that I was beginning to think you might be wondering if this was worth it."

"I don't know where we're headed, but I know I'm not gonna let you go anywhere."

Kyle approached Logan and kissed him tenderly. In that moment, Logan's guilt for not coming clean with Kyle and telling him about his past resurfaced and he felt an urge to tell him everything. But then the moment was gone and he lost himself in Kyle's kiss. Kyle already had enough on his plate with Jessica and Ryan. He didn't want to add more to his worries.

"I don't have to pretend to be straight to have my son," Kyle said. "And you're right. I've been sulking around long enough. It's time to man up and face whatever it is Jessica is sending my way. If she wants a fight, she'll have it."

"Easy there, cowboy," Logan said, smiling. "Keep your weapons holstered a bit longer. You don't know what Jessica will do, so there's no need to put yourself into war mode just yet. Why don't you call her and ask to have Ryan over for the weekend?"

Kyle blinked. "You think I should?"

"Sure. Why not? You're his father and it's been too long since you last saw him."

"But what about you?"

"What about me?"

Kyle hesitated. "I got the impression you weren't exactly crazy about kids."

Logan frowned. "Why?"

"I don't know. I guess I just assumed you weren't exactly the paternal type."

Logan laughed. "I don't know if I'm the paternal type or not, but I can assure you, I don't hate kids. Besides, are you really telling me that you're waiting for my approval to have your kid over for the weekend?"

"Well, no. I was just trying to be considerate."

"Then stop it and go get your kid. Call Jessica, and don't take no for an answer."

Logan watched as Kyle got up from the table and went to call her. He'd never thought of having kids before and he still couldn't see himself raising one. What would he do or say? He knew how much could go wrong and how easy it was to screw things up. He didn't want to have that kind of responsibility on his shoulders. He wouldn't forgive himself if he knew he was responsible for a kid following in his own teenage footsteps. But, then again, this wasn't any kid. This was Kyle's. Would it make any difference? He didn't know how to answer that question.

Logan heard footsteps and looked up. Kyle was back and beaming

"She said 'Yes'."

"She did? That's great news. So when do I get to meet Ryan?" Somewhere inside Logan's head a voice told him he would be a bad example for the kid, but he dismissed it and buried it under the happiness he felt for seeing Kyle so happy.

Kyle sat at the table. "This next weekend, actually."

"Really?"

"Yeah. I couldn't believe it myself. She seemed willing to make a real effort and I didn't even have to argue about being Ryan's father, or having a right to see him."

"I told you she'd come around," Logan said, gently stroking Kyle's arm. "Now, let's eat before this burger gets any colder."

As they ate dinner, Logan thought he should finally come clean with Kyle. He had to tell him about his past. He owed him that. Especially now he was about to play a small part in Ryan's life.

Chapter Twenty-Four

The judge had been staring at Logan with a frown for a while now. He seemed angry but Logan hadn't a clue what was making him mad.

"Are you aware that you messed up? That you wasted the opportunity given to you?" the judge roared, his eyes glinting as if the rage he felt was somehow crystallized in them.

"Your honor, I'm sorry, but I don't know what you're talking about."

The judge grew angrier. His nostrils flared, and his brows were now so furrowed his eyes were barely visible. "How can you claim to love Kyle when you choose to lie to him every day by omitting your filthy secret past? That's a first degree offense! You're hereby sentenced to return to jail."

Logan wanted to say something, anything, but his mouth refused to cooperate. He looked to his side and saw Dave, his former parole officer, waving at him and smiling. Next to him was a shadowy figure whose face Logan couldn't quite make out but who seemed to be laughing.

Finally, he managed to unstick his lips. "But, your honor, I—"

"Take him down!" the judge demanded.

Two guards grabbed Logan by his arms. They were much taller and stronger than he was and lifted him with ease. He looked to Dave again, seeking help, but he wasn't there anymore. In his place stood Kyle, heartbroken, tearing up and silently mouthing the word "Why".

"You should've told me who you were, Logan. You should've," Kyle then kept saying, his disappointed stare burning a hole in Logan's heart.

As Logan was dragged away, he could only think of Kyle and question whether going back to jail was a just price to pay for having been with him. His heart was being squeezed and Logan couldn't breathe anymore.

"Kyle!"

***

"Logan, wake up. You're having one of those nightmares again."

Logan jerked awake and sucked in a quick breath through his teeth. The world unfocused for a moment, but then he saw Kyle's face, worriedly staring at him. His moment of confusion slipped away and he realized it had been the dream that had awakened him. Its delicate fabric was already fraying at the edges, evaporating into oblivion, but the sense of dread it had instilled in Logan remained.

"I'm sorry," Logan said. "Bad dream."

Kyle leaned back on the bed, still gazing at him. "What were you dreaming about this time?"

Logan glanced at Kyle. This was his chance to come clean.

"I don't remember. But I think it had something to do with some war." Logan got out of bed and went straight into the bathroom, navigating around Buddy who was looking up at him, wagging his tail. He stopped in from of the sink, turned the water on and splashed his face. The cold liquid washed away what was left of the dream. Another wasted chance to tell Kyle the truth. Why was he postponing the inevitable? Did he really think Kyle would shun him once he knew about his past? He was a changed man and Kyle would understand. Did he really believe Kyle was so shallow he'd leave him if he knew?

"Are you okay?"

Kyle had just come into the bathroom and was behind Logan, leaning against the door.

"Yes," he said, looking at Kyle's reflection in the bathroom mirror as he dried his face with a towel.

Kyle observed him a moment longer and said, "I'm taking off after breakfast, remember? I have some errands to run in the city before picking up Ryan at Jessica's."

It was one of those days when which day it is doesn't quite register until someone points it out. "Oh, right," Logan said, turning around. "It's Friday. You're coming over after you pick him up, right?"

"No, I think I'm gonna head straight home. I don't plan on arriving too late but it will probably be Ryan's bedtime by then. You can come over, though."

Logan smiled. "I'll let you settle in with Ryan. See you tomorrow morning?"

"I'll text you later, as soon as I get home. In the meantime, we still have bath time for us. And breakfast." Kyle grinned and let his boxer shorts slide to the floor. Logan gazed at Kyle's erection and forgot all about his dream. That could wait.

***

Logan felt nervous. He stood before Kyle's door, wondering if he should go through with this. All the questions he'd had before about being the right man for Kyle were now amplified by the fact he was about to meet Ryan. His mind was fully locked into a circular argument from which only one thought emerged: he had to tell Kyle about his past. Every time he tried to muster up the courage to go through with it, though, something would come up and change his mind. This time, Logan told himself, he couldn't drop such a bomb on Kyle's lap, not just yet. Ryan was there for the first time and he couldn't mess that up. So he knocked and went in, thinking that he'd tell Kyle as soon as Ryan was back to his mother.

"Hello?" Logan called as he closed the door behind him.

"Up here, in Ryan's room."

Logan went up the stairs and found Kyle leaning over a toddler, making silly faces while he changed his diaper. Logan watched him from the door and smiled at the sight. He'd never seen that look of unconditional love in Kyle's eyes before and felt moved by it. The gloss of sadness and worry that Kyle had carried with him since the dinner with Jessica had now gone. In its place was a radiant and palpable happiness that spread in every direction. It touched Logan and made him feel fortunate to be able to share it with Kyle.

"Hey," Kyle said, glancing at Logan. "I'm almost finished. I'm still potty-training Mr. Grumpy, here, and we had a little accident earlier. Didn't we?" Kyle's eyes were again focused on his son.

Ryan's mischievous smile reminded Logan of Kyle. "I think he understood you."

Kyle turned to Logan and laughed. "Of course he did. He's almost two."

Logan raised his eyebrows. "Right. I guess I have much to learn about toddlers," he said, trying not to sound too embarrassed. He was obviously in the dark about small children.

"Don't worry. You'll have plenty of time to catch up." Kyle winked at Logan and then turned to Ryan, who by now was being a little fussy. He picked him up from the changing table and put him on the floor. "We're all set here. Come say 'Hello' to daddy's friend."

Logan stiffened when Kyle stopped in front of him with Ryan. He'd be daddy's "Friend" from now on? He guessed that was the only thing he could be, given how young Ryan was. He shifted his weight to the other leg. He was feeling weirdly uncomfortable around the kid, and it didn't help that Ryan's big, brown eyes pierced him like they could see straight through him and into his soul. He squatted, so Ryan could see him better, then reached for his hand and said, "Hi, Ryan. It's nice to meet you."

Ryan pulled his hand away instinctively and hid behind Kyle's leg, grabbing it with his two tiny arms like his life depended on it. Logan smiled and his heart ached for the kid, despite feeling rejected. He was cute. Not cute in a Buddy sort of way, but Logan was definitely warming to him, even if Ryan seemed able to peruse his soul and judge him for what he'd done in his youth.

"Say 'Hello' to Logan, Ryan. He's a friend." Ryan stayed behind Kyle and said something that sounded like "Scary man". Kyle turned to Logan, who'd now stood up. "I'm sorry. He didn't nap, so he's grumpy and tired. Give me a minute while I put him to bed, okay?"

Logan nodded and left the bedroom. He headed downstairs to the living room, already understanding Kyle's fear of not being a part of Ryan's life. It would be a shame not to see him grow up, despite the risk of being the "Scary man" in that tale.

Fifteen minutes later, Kyle entered the living room. "I'm sorry," he said. "Ryan didn't want to go to sleep."

Logan smiled. "He seems like a nice kid."

"Nice? He's the best one in the entire planet." Kyle chuckled and kissed Logan. "Are you okay? You seem like you have something on your mind. Is it because Ryan thought you were a bad man?"

"No, of course not." Logan almost told him he really was a bad man, or used to be. But it would be selfish of him to spoil Kyle's first evening with his son since leaving Jessica. "I'm just a bit tired, that's all. Almost fell asleep on the couch."

Kyle glanced at his watch. It was almost eight. "You want to take a nap as well, instead of having dinner?" he said, in baby talk.

Logan chuckled and held Kyle closer. "How about we have something to eat before I go home?"

"You're not staying?"

Logan shrugged. "I thought it'd be better for Ryan if I went home. I'm a stranger and it might be weird. You want me to stay?"

"I wanted you to, yes, but my fatherly side tells me you're right." Kyle chuckled. "Man, I hate it that you're right."

Logan laughed. "You should get used to it. I'm never wrong."

"We'll see about that."

During dinner, Logan could see how Kyle was happier than he'd ever seen him since they'd met. The light in his eyes was bright and Kyle spent the entire meal beaming and laughing for no apparent reason. Logan kept smiling and laughing with him, but the more Kyle laughed, the more horrible Logan felt. He'd waited too long to tell him about his past, and the more he waited the more he thought Kyle would perceive it as a betrayal on his part. Kyle would most certainly not want an ex-convict in his house, especially not now Jessica was coming around to the idea of letting Ryan be with his father, when things were tentatively getting back to normal.

He couldn't ruin Kyle's happiness. He wouldn't mess up his relationship with Ryan.

Chapter Twenty-Five

"I'm here," Kyle said from the door.

"I'm gonna be downstairs in a second," Logan answered. He finished drying his hair with a towel, ran his fingers through to comb it and left the bathroom.

Kyle had insisted they should go to the park so he and Ryan could spend some time together and get acquainted. Logan wasn't too sure about this. He was afraid Ryan wouldn't get along with him and wanted to postpone knowing if it was true or not. Or course, he didn't tell Kyle this, so he reluctantly agreed they'd go to the park that day.

"Hey, buddy. And how are you today?" Logan said, crouching in front of Ryan. Buddy woofed at hearing his name, as though upset that someone else could be called it.

Ryan answered with a timid smile.

"Give him a couple of minutes and you should be fine," Kyle said, a huge grin on his lips. "Shall we go?"

"Let me just get my backpack."

Ryan said something and Logan thought it had gone along the lines of "Backpack" and "Wogn", but wasn't sure. His quizzical face was not lost on Kyle, though.

"He said he's also got a backpack, Logan," Kyle chuckled.

Logan laughed and went to the living room. That was a good start. Ryan was no longer hiding behind Kyle's legs and was at least trying to have a conversation with him. He shook his head. The way the little guy had called him "Wogn" and pointed his tiny finger at him was just plain adorable.

When Logan returned to the living room, Ryan and Buddy were playing like they were best friends.

"I'm relieved he doesn't think I'm a bad guy anymore," Logan said after quickly pecking Kyle on the lips, taking advantage of Ryan being distracted by Buddy who was now chasing after him.

"Of course he doesn't. He was just grumpy yesterday. I told you."

The drive to the park was short. They went in Kyle's car because that was where Ryan's child seat was. Buddy sat next to him, peeking out of the window from time to time, thrilled to have a new human in his family. Logan could tell he was really excited. Buddy would normally travel in the car with his head out of the window, trying to catch every scent that swept past. This time, however, he couldn't make up his mind and spent the entire time pushing Ryan with his nose every time he tried to catch his tail, and jumping to the other side of the car to peek outside.

The park was teeming with people that morning. They weren't the only ones who had thought of having a picnic. After parking nearby, Kyle took Ryan out his chair and said, "Don't let him run away. I'll go get his things out of the trunk."

Logan nodded, watching as Ryan scanned the trees and the other kids around him. He was trying to decide if it was better to hold the child's hand or not when Ryan's chubby fingers tried to grab on to his own. Logan smiled without realizing and held on to his tiny hand.

They finally found a fairly empty spot near the pond. It was grassed and under the shade of the trees, which was an added bonus. Logan watched Buddy and Ryan play nearby, vaguely aware of how much his life had changed in such a short time.

"Isn't he the most adorable man you've ever met?" Kyle said.

Logan turned to him, smiling. "He is. Apart from you, of course."

"Of course."

"And look at how happy Buddy is." Logan paused and turned to Kyle. "I really hope you and Jessica can sort things out."

"Me too. But I think we're on the right track… Ryan, no, Ryan. Come here." Kyle quickly stood up and Logan span around to see what was happening. Ryan was chasing after Buddy, the dog now running towards the pond, barking at the ducks.

Adrenaline poured through Logan's veins as he sprang into action, running after them. The memory of the other kid he'd saved from the pond was still fresh in his mind and he feared Buddy would jump into the water and Ryan would go in after him.

"Buddy! Come here!"

Buddy heard him, scrambled to a halt and turned around, tail between his legs, his ears drooping.

"Haven't I told you before? No running after the ducks," he called.

Kyle came back with Ryan in his arms, Buddy slinking at his heels. "Don't run away, okay?" Kyle was telling Ryan.

Logan sighed, only now realizing how fast his heart was thumping. "Jeez. These two scared the hell out of me," he said. "Maybe it wasn't such a good idea to be this close to the pond."

Ryan said something to Kyle while pointing his finger at Buddy. "No, no. Logan's not mad at Buddy," Kyle said. "He was just worried because the pond is dangerous. You can't swim yet, so no running to the pond, okay?"

Ryan nodded.

"I'm glad you're here to translate because I honestly haven't a clue what he's saying half the time."

Kyle chuckled. "You'll get there. Don't worry."

"Maybe we should go for ice cream instead?" Logan said after they had returned to their picnic blanket.

"Let's enjoy ourselves a bit more and then we'll go for ice cream. Relax. You're too wound up. This is perfectly normal with a toddler. As soon as they learn how to walk you have to start worrying about them running away."

Kyle was right. He was too wound up, but he couldn't help it after having watched Ryan run towards the pond.

"This is all new to me, I guess."

"Aww, look at you, worried about our little family. How cute."

There was a moment where they both looked at each other as what Kyle had just said sank in. They both smiled softly. Kyle began teasing Logan but ended up saying something that echoed deep within them both.

"I'm just trying to avoid diving into that pond again. It's disgusting," Logan said, trying to lighten the mood. The thought of being a family with Kyle was one that warmed his heart but it also reminded him of all the stuff he still hadn't come clean about.

The rest of the morning proved calmer, the only noteworthy event being Ryan smearing ice cream all over himself. Kyle and Logan couldn't help but laugh at his surprised face when he realized he was then all out of ice cream. Most of it was now on his clothes. But who could be mad at the little guy? As is the way with kids, though, he quickly forgot about it and was soon asking if he could play with Buddy again.

***

The next day dawned hot and beautiful. Logan had had trouble sleeping. He felt guilty for everything he was still keeping from Kyle. This, in turn, wouldn't let his mind wind down and he ended up waking up in the early hours of the morning. He went for a run to try to relax, but only managed to arrive home all sweaty and with a headache. He was coming out of the shower when he heard Kyle calling for him downstairs.

"I'm really, really sorry to ask you this, but could you please look after Ryan for a couple of hours? I have a bit of an emergency with that project I'm working on. The client called me last night. He forgot that he also needs business cards, and needs them ASAP. It's always the same. The clients screws up I end up putting in the extra hours."

Logan held the towel he'd wrapped around his waist with one hand while gazing at a distressed Kyle. Ryan was already playing with Buddy and ignoring them both.

"Can't I go to your home and stay there while you work? I'm not sure I can look after him on my own. What if something happens?" Logan was panicking but tried not to show it.

"The client wants to Skype with me. He's really good at nitpicking and I can't risk Ryan having a fit while I'm trying to address his concerns. You'll be fine. I packed a bag with everything you need," and Kyle handed Logan a heavy bag. "It'll be a couple of hours, tops. Please?"

How could he say no? "Let me just change. I'll be right back," Logan said, smiling. He was terrified of being alone with Ryan, though. He feared he'd mess up and injure him. Weren't children really frail? What if Ryan broke an arm under his watch or ate something he shouldn't? But he kept his fears to himself and returned five minutes later to a relieved Kyle who couldn't stop thanking him.

"Thank you, thank you, thank you!" he kept saying. "I promise I'll make it up to you."

Kyle left without saying "Goodbye" to Ryan. He didn't want the boy to start crying over it. With any luck, he'd continue playing with Buddy and not notice anything until much later. Logan closed the front door behind Kyle and went to the living room where Ryan was chasing after Buddy. You got this, he thought, placing the bag Kyle had brought on the couch. He sat and rummaged through it, taking note of everything inside. He was expecting to find at least a book on how to take care of toddlers without killing them, but the bag had nothing of sort. Only diapers, baby wipes, food and a number of toys.

Logan knew Ryan was being potty-trained but Kyle hadn't brought any potty with him. He panicked for a moment. How the hell was he supposed to let the kid take a piss? But then he took a deep breath and decided to cross that bridge if he came to it.

Ryan stopped chasing after Buddy and looked around. "Dada?" He toddled toward Logan, his big round eyes focused only on him. "Dada?" he said again, pointing his little, chubby finger at him.

"Daddy will be right back," Logan said with a big smile as he leaned forward. He felt like a giant in front of Ryan. "Go play with Buddy a bit more."

Ryan's little face grew scared and his mouth began working. Logan couldn't make much of his gibberish but he was certain he'd heard something along the lines of "I want dada, or else". Of course, the kid wasn't really making any threats, but Logan was sure it was the tone of a child who was beginning to feel scared about not having his parents around. Logan crouched, his mind racing to come up with something with which he could distract Ryan.

"Buddy, go get your ball." Buddy, who had been right behind Ryan, as though on guard, raised his ears and tilted his head. "Go get the ball," Logan said again, and Buddy left the living room running. Ryan was still making a whole case about why he wanted his daddy, in a language that was somehow a mixture of words that reminded Logan of English and something else he wasn't entirely sure off. Logan thought that two-year olds were more articulate than this. But, then again, Ryan wasn't two yet.

Buddy came into the living room again, a ball in his mouth. He let it fall to the floor at Logan's feet and then yapped excitedly. Logan grabbed the ball and showed it to Ryan.

"Look, Ryan. Watch Buddy." Ryan followed his hand and watched him throw the ball into the hall. Buddy bolted into action and chased after it, claws clicking on and scratching the wooden floor. Logan thought he would later regret playing ball with Buddy inside the house, but he had panicked.

His strategy seemed to pay off. Ryan was now clapping and giggling as he watched Buddy sliding across the floor, trying to stop before hitting the wall. Buddy snatched the ball and came back to the living room. He gave the ball back to Logan and started to bark, asking for more.

"Wanna try, Ryan?" Ryan held the ball with both hands, his fingers too small. "Now, throw it."

Ryan flexed both his tiny arms and threw the ball, jumping at the same time. It was a good first effort, but the ball barely rolled away from them. Buddy watched, puzzled, as the ball rolled just a couple of feet, then went to retrieve it in a much more leisurely fashion. He somehow seemed to know that Ryan was different from Logan, and that playing with him required a different approach. He trotted calmly to the ball, picked it up and returned, dropping it at Ryan's feet. After licking his own nose a couple of times, he nudged Ryan into picking up the ball. Ryan giggled, picked it up and threw it again.

Logan drew in a deep breath and silently walked over to the couch, watching them play and feeling proud for having managed to avoid his first child-related crisis. Having a kid wasn't that bad, now was it?

***

"What's the matter, Ryan?"

Logan's question was met with more crying. Ryan had been inconsolable for the past half an hour, screaming bloody murder and seemingly unable to express himself in any other way. Logan was getting desperate. He'd tried giving him food, making silly faces, throwing Buddy's ball, but nothing had worked. It had been nearly three hours since Kyle had dropped Ryan off and Logan could only think that Kyle was running late. He didn't know what else he could do, and didn't want to call Kyle and risk interrupting his meeting.

In an act of desperation, Logan picked Ryan up and held him in his arms. He'd been avoiding touching Ryan too much as he didn't know what the boundaries were. He was also afraid of hurting him and so had been dancing around the poor kid since he'd arrived—and especially since the tantrum had begun. Logan held him close, realizing how small and light he was. Of course he knew this, but it was completely different from having the actual experience of holding him. Logan began humming a tune but Ryan kept crying and talking gibberish. He could feel Ryan's warmth in his arms, the little guy's heart pounding away against his chest. He never realized how quickly toddler's hearts pumped. It was like holding a little scared bird. Ryan also smelled of baby shampoo and something else, like moisturizing cream. Suddenly, Logan wanted to protect Ryan from the world, to keep him in his arms and hold him throughout his life. He kept hold of him in one arm and, with his free hand, rummaged through the bag Kyle had brought, trying to find a pacifier. He found it and attempted to give it to Ryan, who avoided it a couple of times. He was rubbing his eyes, clearly tired and sleepy. Logan insisted and Ryan finally calmed down a bit and took the pacifier, sucking on it while his eyelids grew heavier. Logan kept rocking him in his arms while humming some tune he wasn't too sure was a real song, holding on to Ryan like he was the most precious gift in the world. Ryan eventually fell asleep, but Logan continued to cradle him, not wanting to let go.

Kyle walked in and Logan signaled for him to be quiet.

"Is he sleeping?" Kyle whispered, a broad smile on his face.

"Yes, after having had a fit for God knows how long."

Kyle chuckled and pecked Logan on his lips. "Thank you for doing this. You'd be an excellent father."

Logan felt warm and fuzzy on the inside at the image it conjured in his mind. Would he, really? "You're just buttering me up. How was it?"

Kyle sighed. "I managed to finish everything, after having to listen to the guy nitpicking about things that were perfect two days ago."

Logan smiled. "I'm sorry."

"Fortunately, the project is done now and I don't have to deal with him anymore." Kyle reached his arms out for Ryan but Logan resisted for a moment. He didn't want to let him go. It was so good to hold him in his arms, to feel his heartbeat and listen to his rhythmic breathing.

"Are you driving him to Jessica's?" Logan asked, now watching Ryan asleep in Kyle's arms.

"Yeah. Hopefully, he'll be asleep the whole trip." Kyle kissed Logan. "I have to run if I want to avoid traffic. See you at dinner?"

Logan smiled. "It's a date."

They kissed again and Logan watched as Kyle put Ryan in the SUV's child seat and finally drove away. Somehow he felt complete, more determined than ever to come clean to Kyle and do whatever it took not to lose him.

Chapter Twenty-Six

The day had arrived. No more postponing, no more coming up with excuses. He was going to come clean with Kyle about who he was and what had happened in his past. For the past couple of weeks Logan had gone back and forth in his head over telling Kyle about his time in prison and all the stupid mistakes he'd made in his past, but when he got to the part where he actually had to open his mouth and tell him everything he had rehearsed, he'd got cold feet. He feared Kyle would look at him differently and walk away; he worried that he was being selfish and would ruin the only time he'd seen Kyle happy, now he was able to spend some quality time with Ryan; but most of all he feared Kyle wouldn't forgive him for not having been truthful from the beginning.

Kyle was due to arrive soon with Ryan. Jessica had agreed to let Kyle have him again for the weekend and he was over the moon. Logan felt terrible that he was about to burst his happy bubble, but he couldn't postpone it any longer. Every day that passed by without telling him seemed like a lie and it was corroding him on the inside. He had to tell Kyle. He just had to. And he would, as soon as he arrived to have lunch.

Someone rapped on the door and Buddy started barking. Logan snapped back from his thoughts. That was weird. Kyle never knocked before coming in. By the time Logan got to the front door, Buddy was barking defensively.

"Buddy, shush," he said. Buddy looked at him, his barks dwindling into a low growl. "What's wrong with you? Don't do that." Buddy stayed silent after that, and then the rapping returned. Logan opened the door. On the other side stood a rotund man, probably in his fifties, a cowboy hat on his head and an unkempt mustache blooming in every direction from under his nose. Logan was undecided as to whether the man was trying to grow it or was just too cheap to buy some scissors.

"Can I help you?"

"Logan Moore?" the man asked. He seemed annoyed.

"Yes."

"I'm Bill Chase, your new parole officer. May I come in?"

Before Logan could answer, Bill barged into the house like he owned the place and began scanning it, as if expecting to find something.

"Come on in," Logan said, despite being displeased with the man's attitude. So this was his new parole officer. He'd wondered what had taken them so long, but at least he was finally here. For a moment, he resented Dave for not having called him about this new fellow, but he immediately felt bad. The last time they'd spoken, Dave had implied he was having heart problems, so probably had more pressing matters. "I didn't know you were coming. Did you try to call?" He knew perfectly well the guy hadn't.

Bill turned to Logan, grabbed his belt buckle and tilted his head. He looked like a cowboy assessing how to lasso a calf. "No. I like to make a surprise visit on my first day and see what kind of trouble I'm dealing with."

Trouble he's dealing with? Now that was a fine way of judging people ahead of time. Logan got the feeling that this Bill character was one of those who liked their position of power a bit too much. He'd have to be careful.

Buddy began a low growl, his eyes sharply focused on the guy and his ears flat against his head. Bill was watching him nervously.

"Are you gonna control that mutt or do I have to put it in my report that you have a menacing dog?"

Logan decided to play along, for now. Bill was definitely not like Dave and clearly enjoyed being a dick. There was nothing Logan could do, really. His future depended on the report Bill was going to write and so he would just have to put up with him.

"Buddy, shush. Go to the living room. Go on."

Buddy looked at Logan but then did as asked. The man let out a sigh of relief but tried to hide it.

"Good. Now, control your dog while I search your house."

"Search my house? Why?"

Bill smirked. "Why not? Do you have anything to hide?"

"Of course not, but Dave never acted like I was a criminal."

"Well, that's Dave's shortcoming, since you are a criminal. Stay with your dog while I do my job. I may have a few questions for you afterwards."

Logan's blood boiled. He tried to control himself, not to show just how much he really wanted to smack Bill in his stupid little mustache. "No. This is my house. I'll come with you and show you around."

Bill squinted and shrugged, and Logan was relieved to hear him agree, concerned he might try planting false evidence somewhere. He sure looked shady enough to try something like that.

For the first time since leaving jail, Logan felt utterly vulnerable. The man seemed to dislike him for no reason other than having been in jail. He also got this vibe that Bill would much prefer it if Logan went back there.

"Wow. This is a big knife, isn't it? You like to cook?" Bill said after a couple of minutes searching the kitchen. He was wielding one of Logan's chef's knives, which had just been lying on the counter.

Logan wasn't sure where he was heading with this. "Actually, I do."

Bill opened a drawer. "My, my. So many knives. You do seem to like them big time. And sharpened," he added, running a finger across one of the blades. "You should be careful about having so many with you. Some people might think you're up to no good. You know, having been in prison and all."

"I'd have to be really stupid to go on a killing spree with one of those." Logan stopped talking, fearing he'd said too much, but he was getting really mad at Bill and his idiotic innuendos.

Bill scoffed, closed the drawer and continued searching the kitchen. He then rummaged under the sink and a minute later came up with a bottle in his hand, a furious expression on his face. "Are you trying to go back to jail?"

Logan blinked at the guy. He was holding the drain cleaner. "What? No. Why would I?"

"Then why do you have in your possession something that can be made into an explosive?"

Logan blinked again. Drain cleaner could be used for that? "I have no idea what you're talking about. Did you at least read my file? Do you know I was in jail for robbing rich people? As in breaking in through windows and such? I use the drain cleaner to clean the drain!" Logan was talking a bit louder than he wanted to but couldn't contain himself. The man was an idiot.

"Please lower your voice or I'll have to report you get agitated easily."

Bill resumed his hunt around the house, and after almost forty-five excruciating minutes, involving lots of stops and stupid questions, finally seemed satisfied with himself and was ready to leave. Logan walked him to the front door. Buddy returned from the living room and sat by Logan's side, clearly having had enough of keeping out of the way. Logan let him stay. He felt aggravated by this little man who held so much power over him. So Logan was beginning to enjoy seeing him start to sweat as Buddy focused his gaze on him.

"I'll be going to have a talk this Monday with your boss." Bill paused, but Logan said nothing. "I just hope for your sake you still have a job."

"Don't worry, I got promoted recently," Logan said, coolly.

Bill lifted an eyebrow, about to speak when Kyle opened the front door, holding Ryan by his tiny hand. Logan felt his stomach sink.

"Hey, I hope lunch's ready—oh, sorry. I didn't know you had company," Kyle said, looking from Bill to Logan, a silent question in his eyes.

Logan's heart raced. His past had caught up with him before he'd even had a chance to come clean about it. And before he could say something, Bill stepped in front of Logan and faced Kyle.

"Hi. I'm Bill Chase, Logan's parole officer," he said, offering his hand. "For how long have you known each other?"

Kyle recoiled. "Maybe three months, I guess. I'm sorry, what's going on?" Kyle was now staring at Logan, confusion plastered all over his face.

Logan was lost for words. This was not the way he'd envisioned telling him.

"I see Mr. Moore didn't tell you about his condition." Bill looked over his shoulder at Logan and then focused his gaze back on Kyle. "Well, he should've. He knows better. Logan was released from jail about nine months ago, on good behavior, and I'm here to ensure he's complying with the conditions of his release."

Bill's words punched Logan in his gut and the room became blurry. Kyle seemed unsure if he was being pranked or not. His face momentarily twitched into an awkward smile, but then turned into concern. "Is this some kind of joke?"

"Dadda, dadda." Ryan was pulling Kyle's hand and doing a little dance, getting bored and wanting attention. Kyle picked him up.

"I can assure you, sir, this is no joke," Bill said, showing him his badge.

Kyle's eyes briefly widened. "Why didn't you tell me?" he said, looking at Logan, a sense of betrayal creeping across his face.

Logan wanted to say there'd been nothing he'd wanted more, but got scared he wouldn't understand, wouldn't understand that it had all happened a lifetime ago, that he was now a different man. He wanted to tell Kyle that the connection he'd felt between them since the day they'd first met ran deeper than anything he'd ever felt before and that he'd been dreading this day, fearing Kyle would go away, breaking his heart in the process. Logan wanted to tell him all of this but somehow couldn't. His tongue didn't want to obey him, and it didn't help that Bill kept staring at him like he was highly amused.

"Well, you seem to have a lot on your plate right now," Bill said, a disgusted twitch on his nose. "I'll pay you a visit at work come Monday," and with this, he left.

A heavy silence fell between Logan and Kyle, punctuated by Ryan's attention grabbing gibberish.

"I was going to tell you. I've been postponing it for so long," Logan said.

"So why didn't you?"

Logan shifted his weight from one leg to the other. "I was afraid you'd leave."

"You were afraid I'd leave? Why?"

"Because every time people find out about me I see the way they look at me. They change and I was afraid you'd change too."

Kyle furrowed his eyebrows. "You think I'm that shallow?"

"No. Of course not. And I know you wanted to know more about my past. And I wanted to tell you everything, I did, but this isn't something you share with someone on a first date. It's not like I was afraid you wouldn't like me for not caring about ice cream. It's bit bigger than that."

"You kept this from me every time I asked you about your life, even though I've shared everything with you, Logan. Everything. Jessica, Ryan, my fears, everything. And you kept this to yourself? Have you ever thought that maybe people leave you not because of your past but because you don't share yourself with them? Because you don't trust people enough? I thought we were in this together." Kyle turned around and opened the door to leave.

"Wait," Logan said. "Where are you going?"

"I have to go. I have Ryan with me. I can't be here right now. I have to go."

"Please, stay."

But Kyle only briefly looked over his shoulder before he left.

Chapter Twenty-Seven

"Go play with Fuzzy while daddy makes lunch, okay?"

Ryan babbled on about how he and Fuzzy were hungry and turned his attention to the couple of stuffed toys Kyle had placed for him on a matt on the kitchen floor. Kyle gazed at his son toddling towards the corner and sighed. He turned around and opened the fridge but was left staring at the food for a couple of seconds. He'd forgotten why he'd opened it, his brain tuned in to the talk he'd just had with Logan. His chest was compressed by a pain he didn't want to explore right now. Kyle shook his head and focused on what he had to do: prepare Ryan's lunch. Then he had to take a nap, and then… Well, he didn't know what he was doing then, but he also didn't want to think about that right now. Right now, he had to find something for Ryan's lunch. He scanned the fridge again.

There weren't many options as they were supposed to have been eating at Logan's. Kyle had a soup he'd made the previous day and some chicken. He picked up both and poured them into the blender. As the machine whirred loudly and pureed the meat, blending it with the soup, his mind drifted again to what had just happened. He was having a hard time digesting it all. How could Logan have lied to him? And if he had succeeded in omitting such an important aspect of his life, what else could he be lying about? Kyle no longer knew if he could trust Logan. Had he been taking advantage of him? Was Kyle an easy target for having come out so recently? Was that why Logan was with him? Kyle's memories took him back to their first kiss, their weekend away in the cabin, the first time they had had sex, and his gut churned at the thought that it could all have been a giant lie.

Kyle snapped back into reality and turned the blender off. Soup with chicken wasn't going to earn him any father-of-the-year awards but it was the best he could concoct in such short notice. He poured a portion into a glass bowl and microwaved it for a minute. Even he knew better than to heat food in plastic containers. After the microwave dinged, he took the bowl out and poured a smaller portion into a plastic dish shaped like a smiley face, so Ryan could eat it by himself. Ryan really enjoyed eating off this plate.

"Come on, Ryan. Lunch's ready."

Ryan ran to the table and Kyle helped him climb onto his chair. Logan's desperate eyes popped up in Kyle's mind again but he ignored them and focused on his son. He would put him to nap after lunch, play with him after he woke up and put that morning's events into a box he'd then lock and throw away the key.

***

The doorbell rang and Kyle's whole body tensed up. He wasn't ready to talk with Logan and to listen to what he had to say. But Ryan was still sleeping and he didn't want to risk him waking up. He'd better open the door before Logan rang the bell again.

"Jessica? What are you doing here?"

Jessica stood there, a timid smile blooming on her face. "You forgot Ryan's blanky, and you know how cranky he gets at night without it."

That was true but Ryan also had Fuzzy to sleep with when blanky wasn't around. It was hard to believe she'd driven all the way up here just to bring them a blanket. Kyle looked at her. She seemed uneasy.

"Come in." Kyle closed the door behind her and they both went into the living room. "He's still sleeping." Jessica smiled and grabbed Ryan's security blanket from her big bag.

"In any case, here."

Kyle took the blanket. "Did you really drive three hours just to bring me this? You know I have Fuzzy here."

"You do? Oh, that's right. Ryan left it here the other day." Jessica shrugged. "Better be safe than sorry, right?" She smiled nervously and looked around.

"Are you okay?"

Jessica took in a deep breath. "Actually, I'm here to invite you to dinner."

"You drove all the way up here to invite me to dinner? Are you sure you're okay?"

"I… " Jessica turned her eyes away from Kyle while squeezing her fingers. She perched herself on the couch and looked at Kyle again. "I need to tell you something. Remember Andy?"

Remember? How could he forget him? Andy had appeared at his house just after he'd told Jessica the truth, wanting to punch him on the nose to avenge her honor.

"How could I forget him?" he said, trying to sound light about it. In reality, he just wanted to kick the idiot in the balls. He sat across from her, a bad feeling growing in his stomach.

"He's…been helping me get through this. And the other day we had this moment and we kind of kissed."

Kyle's eyes widened for a moment. Had he heard her right? She'd kissed that jerk? He felt a hint of something similar to jealousy but decided to ignore it. "You kissed him?" What was he supposed to say? "Do you like him?"

Jessica squirmed on the couch and cleared her throat. "I don't know." She sighed. She seemed miserable. "The truth is… The truth is that shortly after you came out to me, he and I… He and I started seeing each other."

Kyle frowned, trying to process what she was telling him. "Wait, you've been seeing Andy?" Now that was something he wasn't expecting to hear. Especially not after the scene she had made the night she found out about Logan. He didn't know what to make of it, or whether he should feel angry or not. Jessica was admitting to having an affair with another man, but he wasn't exactly in a position to demand anything from her. Nor did he want to.

"Yes. Look, I feel terrible about it and that's why I told him we should stop seeing each other, at least for now. It all began because I felt betrayed and miserable, and he was there to offer a shoulder I could cry on. I guess it also helped I've always known he's had a crush on me. It felt good to know I was still desirable." Jessica looked at the ceiling and shook her head. "Oh, my gosh! I'm such a loser!"

Kyle smiled. "So when you accused me of cheating on you with Logan you were really just being crazy out of guilt?" Kyle chuckled. Somehow it all seemed funny, in a tragic, Greek kind of way. "Couldn't you have chosen someone…better?"

"I didn't choose him. It happened. And it was only a couple of times."

"I'm sorry. It was a joke. I shouldn't be joking. And you shouldn't have driven up here just to apologize for it. You don't owe me anything, Jess." His tone was of sadness, but she really didn't owe him anything. And he wasn't sure why he was sad about it. Their marriage had been over for a long time.

"We're still technically married."

"Consider us even, then."

Jessica smiled. "I'm sorry I assaulted Logan. And I'm sorry I acted like a crazy person at that dinner."

"Don't be. Water under the bridge. We should be looking forward, to the future, not to what we've done. We've both made mistakes."

"Can I buy you dinner? You can bring Logan if you want."

Jessica's words punched Kyle in his gut. He was having a hard time disguising his sadness over what had happened that morning, and her mentioning Logan finally cracked the glass from which he'd built his meagre defenses. "I don't think I'll be bringing Logan along."

"Is he working? Maybe another day, then?"

Kyle wasn't sure he should tell her about what had happened. It was awkward, to say the least. But he was also in desperate need of talking with someone and Jessica had been his best friend up until recently. "No. Actually, I'm not sure we're together anymore." Kyle told her everything. By the end, Jessica was looking at him with an open mouth.

"But what was he in jail for?" she said after a moment of silence when neither she nor Kyle knew what to say.

"I don't even know."

"You didn't ask?"

Kyle realized he hadn't. In fact, in the heat of the moment the only thing that had crossed his mind was accusing Logan of being secretive about his past, and then leaving, of course. "No."

"Why not? Don't you want to know what happened?" Jessica seemed bewildered.

"Of course I do, but I felt betrayed. I was in shock and only wanted to leave."

Jessica raised her eyebrows. "The universe works in mysterious ways," she said, a hint of a smile on her face.

"What do you mean?"

Jessica sighed. "Not too long ago I was in your exact same position. I too felt betrayed, not knowing what to do, but in the meantime I've learned that as distressed as you might feel right now, turning your back on Logan without listening to what he has to say will just hurt you in the long run."

She was right but he wasn't ready to listen to any of it. "He had enough time to come clean with me. Why didn't he?"

"You mean, like you had years to talk with me about being gay?" Kyle pursed his lips, and Jessica, probably feeling she was being misunderstood, said, "Look, I'm not attacking you or even accusing you of anything. I'm just reminding you that coming to terms with our own truths is not easy. You said that to me. Remember?"

He remembered. He just didn't know it would come around to bite him in his ass this quickly.

"Whatever it was that Logan did, I can assure you he's a good man," Jessica said, with a certainty of someone who'd known him for years.

"What makes you so sure of it?"

"By the way he talks about you, the way he looks at you. He's a kind, gentle soul, and you know it. You should talk to him. See what he has to say before you say or do something you'll regret. I bet you're already imagining all these scenarios about him being a murderer when he could just have been in the wrong place at the wrong time."

Kyle shuffled on the couch. "I'm not imaging anything." He was, but he didn't feel comfortable admitting it. Jessica knew him too well.

"Okay," she said, smiling. "But just listen to him, already, and wait until then to decide on whether you'll forgive him or not."

Chapter Twenty-Eight

After Kyle left, Logan thought of going after him but the shame that oozed throughout his body prevented him from moving. As he listened to Kyle's SUV leaving, his gut froze and he couldn't stop shivering despite the afternoon's heat. Buddy stayed besides him, his low whine giving away that he was worried. However much Logan wanted to reassure Buddy everything was fine, he just couldn't. Buddy always read beyond his attempts at smiling.

Instead of going after Kyle, he went into his garage and dove headfirst into work. He had always hidden behind physical chores whenever he wanted to forget something. A couple of hours sweating and he would emerge as good as new, he told himself. So, Logan sawed and hammered all afternoon, only this time, no matter how hard he worked, he couldn't forget Kyle's disappointed face. He finally gave up and threw the hammer to one side. It banged into a pile of debris and it all came crashing down with a loud noise that startled Buddy. He came up to Logan with an expression of mild disapproval in his eyes. He woofed, as if to say enough was enough.

Logan spent that night tossing and turning , unable to sleep. He kept thinking back to what had happened, especially the expression of betrayal on Kyle's face, and feared he would never want to see him again. He got out of bed at sunrise. If he couldn't sleep, he might as well do something productive. He went for a run, trying to calm his mind and shut down his thoughts. He was still debating whether he should go after Kyle or give him some space. But he wasn't one just to give up. Kyle should know the whole story before deciding Logan wasn't worth his time. True as that might be, Logan still didn't want to cause a scene with Ryan around. And the kid would be there for the weekend.

After returning home and showering, Logan prepared some scrambled eggs and black coffee for breakfast. His morning run had left him tired and starving, and although he wasn't anywhere near reaching a conclusion about what to do, at least he had his appetite. He took this as a good sign, then went outside to his porch swing and sat down to eat. The morning was silent apart from the birds singing and the gentle breeze ruffling the dead leaves and swaying the trees. Logan let the beauty of the view setting in as he ate.

Buddy woofed and Logan snapped out of his trance. He turned to his faithful friend and saw he was standing up, his ears firmly pointed forward. He woofed again and Logan followed where he was looking. He heard a car approaching and a moment later saw a grey SUV.

It was Kyle.

Logan's heart rushed into a frenzy and rapped against his chest. He wasn't ready to see him, not just yet, his thoughts still all over the place, but Kyle was already stepping out of his car and approaching the house. Logan straightened himself and placed his scrambled eggs on the bench. Kyle's lips were pursed and there was a seriousness about him that made Logan's gut churn. Buddy was barking excitedly at Kyle, jumping around him like he'd been away for ages.

Kyle climbed the three steps to the porch, petted Buddy and looked at Logan, hands now deep into his pockets. "Hi," he said. His forehead was marred by a couple of wrinkles and he seemed self-conscious. "Can we talk?"

Logan nodded. "Where's Ryan?"

"He's with Jessica. She came over yesterday and ended up staying the night." Logan's eyes widened in surprise but he said nothing. Kyle then sighed. "Anyway, I just wanted to say...to say that I don't think I handled the situation very well yesterday."

"You think?" Logan said on an impulse, but soon regretted it.

Kyle frowned. "Yes, I think I could've handled it better, but I wasn't exactly expecting to have someone tell me that the person I thought I knew suddenly has this big, giant aspect to his life that he's kept a secret."

"And what was I supposed to do, Kyle? Finish our beers the first time we were at the bar and you said to me you were gay with an 'Oh, and by the way, I did some pretty stupid things when I was younger and ended up in jail'. Was that it?"

"I don't know, but yes, you could've said something. You had plenty of time."

"Like you had all those years to come clean to Jessica about being gay?" Logan was breathing hard now, angry at Kyle for making him hear the truth he didn't want to hear. But he didn't want to fight. And he didn't want to hurt him. Kyle was wide-eyed and flushed. He seemed furious. "I'm sorry. I...I didn't mean that. I know how hard it must've been for you."

Kyle sighed, deeply, and leaned against the porch railing. "Jessica told me the exact same thing," he said in a low voice.

"What?"

"I was going on and on, angry about you having not shared your past with me. I told her you'd had enough time to come clean and she said the exact same thing to me, reminded me of the years I'd kept her in the dark." Kyle's gaze lay somewhere off in the distance, way beyond the house, but then he turned to Logan. "I came here to apologize for the way I left yesterday. I should've listened to what you had to say but I felt overwhelmed and had to go. I acted like a diva. Somehow we ended up fighting. I'm sorry."

"No, I'm sorry for the way I just spoke to you. You didn't deserve that."

Kyle smiled. "How about we stop with the apologies? Huh?"

Logan nodded. "Okay. So, is there anything you would like to know?"

"Can you tell me what happened?"

Logan sighed, his gaze lost somewhere on the wooden floor. "You know what one of my first memories is? Me shaking my mother's shoulder, trying to wake her up and thinking she was sick. She wasn't. She was just passed out from drinking. I was five or six. My home wasn't exactly a welcoming place for children. I don't really know if she loved me or if I was just a burden, but I'm guessing it was the latter." Logan scoffed. "I was probably just the stupid kid who soaked up all her money on food and clothes when she could have been buying more booze."

Logan paused, intertwining and rubbing his fingers nervously. "Between my drunken mother and my crime-ridden neighborhood, I was caught in a series of missteps that led me to a life of crime. I used to hang around on the streets all the time, and my—shall we call them—friends started challenging me to tag along with them on their 'opportunities' to make easy money. They would spot mansions where their owners were away, vacationing or something, and have me open the houses for them. I was young and small back then, could squeeze into anywhere, even the weirdest places. As I grew up, the challenges grew as well, and soon I was robbing not so empty places. By then I was perfectly aware of what I was doing. I'm not trying to make excuses. But I was also really angry at life, and, well, acting out was the only way I had to blow off some steam. So, I ended up robbing people, rich people. It was stupid, but I decided I wouldn't take from those who were as poor as I was." Logan scoffed again. "I guess it was a childish way of justifying my acts as something commendable."

Logan sighed and straightened himself. He glanced at Kyle but quickly looked away, fearing he'd shocked him too much, maybe made him disgusted at his story. But he wasn't finished. "By the time I was twenty, I'd already had my fair share of encounters with the law. This was also around the time an associate of mine managed to persuade me to rob some mansion he'd heard about. I should've said 'No', but deep down I guess I wanted to do something stupid enough to get caught. The whole thing went terribly wrong because the owner was in the house when he was supposed to be away. My associate assaulted him and neither of us knew that a silent alarm had been set off the minute we'd stepped into the house. The police arrived and caught us red-handed. Our sentence was harsh on account of the aggravated assault, but they released me after five years for good conduct. During my time there I grew a lot. I took advantage of the prison's library to read everything I could, took a couple of courses and end up falling in love with carpentry."

Logan let out a long breath. "I didn't tell you about my past because I was afraid you wouldn't be able to see beyond it. Since I got out I've grown accustomed to being rejected because of it. I've been to a lot of job interviews, believe me, seen the interviewers' faces subtly change from interest to fear the moment my past came out . Then I came to Greenville. This town was really a lifesaver. It made it possible for me to start over without my past dragging me down. I wanted to tell you. I really did."

Logan at last plucked up the courage to lift his chin and look at Kyle. He seemed sad, but at least he now knew everything there was to know. No more lies, no more avoiding talking about his past. He hoped Kyle would see past it, but, if not, Logan would have to accept it and move on with his life.

It was Kyle's turn to sigh. "And here was I, moping about my problems and my life. I feel so embarrassed." He approached Logan and sat on the porch swing, by his side. "I'm so sorry for having rambled on about my privileged life and forcing you to hear it. My problems are meaningless when compared to yours. I'm just another case of a poor-little-white-man moping around for not being happy. Who cares?"

Logan blinked, dumbfounded but also excited at the same time. Kyle didn't seem to care about his stupid mistakes. "Don't be silly. And please, don't compare your problems with mine. The difficulties you went through are every bit as valid as mine. You don't have to be the most miserable person on earth for your problems to be worth it."

"I guess you're right," Kyle said, scratching his forehead. He went quiet for a moment, his eyes lost in Logan's. "I'm sorry you went through all that. I really am."

"It's all in the past now," Logan said with a shrug.

"Do you know where your parents are?"

"No, and honestly it doesn't matter. I stopped hoping for a normal family long ago." Seeing Kyle's demeanor change into one of sadness, Logan quickly added: "But don't feel bad. I'm not. I know how this can sound, but it really doesn't bother me anymore. I spent too long trying to connect with my mother. Some things are not meant to be and she wasn't meant to be a parent."

Kyle said nothing. Instead, he leaned over and kissed Logan, a gentle brush of lips that quickly transformed into an urgent kiss conveying how much they'd missed each other despite being apart for less than a day. The surprise Logan felt by Kyle's move quickly went away. He grabbed Kyle by the small of his back and pulled him closer, fearing he'd run away again. The previous afternoon had forced him to imagine every possible scenario without Kyle, every way in which his life would be void of happiness, the broken heart he'd spend months mending. Kyle had made him believe he could be happy and normal, someone worthy of being loved, and so Logan hugged him closer and kissed him harder in a bid to cast away the dread that had been spreading in his gut since the previous afternoon. Kyle climbed on top of Logan and slid his hands under his T-shirt, exploring his torso from waist to upper chest, feeling his muscles and making Logan's skin gather into goosebumps. Kyle pulled Logan's T-shirt over his head and threw it aside. Then, he kissed him on his pecs and licked his nipples, his tongue playing with them and making Logan feel an urgent need somewhere inside. He couldn't pinpoint exactly where the urge arose, only knew he was feeling it throughout his body, a thirst that engulfed him and made him writhe. His penis reacted and grew hard against his shorts, pressing against Kyle.

"I want you," Kyle said.

Logan smiled. "Hold on." He grabbed Kyle's legs and got up, wanting to carry him inside, but Kyle was almost as tall as him and his legs faltered. "I didn't think this through," he said, laughing, while Kyle hopped off him to the ground.

"Guess not," Kyle said, grinning.

Logan held his hand and dragged him into the house and up to the bedroom. They stripped each other frantically, drunk on desire. Kyle kneeled down and took Logan's cock in his mouth, bobbing back and forth, sucking him like it held the key to quench his thirst. Logan's breathing became labored as he held on to Kyle's head. He almost let himself go with the sensual wave that washed over him as Kyle's tongue twirled around the crown of his cock.

"Easy there or I'm gonna come," he said in between ragged breaths.

"Don't you wanna?"

"Yes, but I also want to keep going."

They both grinned and Kyle stood up and kissed Logan. Kyle ground his penis against Logan's, own white-hot and throbbing one. Then Logan grabbed them both. It was so good to have them in his hand and feel their meaty volume filling it. Logan circled his thumb around both crowns, spreading precum on them. Surges of electricity ran through his body. Kyle whimpered. They both breathed raggedly and fast while kissing, barely able to contain their lust. Their dance led them to the bed, where they fell over each other, lips almost as one.

"Hold on," Logan said. He reached to his nightstand and opened the drawer, searching for a condom and lube. "Here," he said, giving it to Kyle. "I think you're ready."

Kyle gazed at the condom and then at Logan. "Are you sure? I thought that you'd be the one to...you know."

"To what?"

"Be the giver?"

Logan chuckled. "Remember how we talked about this being whatever we wanted it to be?" Logan winked and gave the condom to Kyle, who ripped the package open and put it on. Logan guided Kyle through the process of applying generous amounts of lube, then said, "Now, go about it slowly."

Kyle nodded and Logan splayed his legs, inviting him over. He felt Kyle's cock tentatively brushing his hole and gasped.

"I'm sorry. Did I hurt you?" Kyle asked, worry creases marring his forehead.

"What? No! Shut up and keep going," and a mischievous grin spread across his lips.

Kyle grabbed one of Logan's legs and, again with his hand, guided his cock. He brushed Logan's hole one more time and again Logan moaned and bit his lips. He couldn't remember the last time he'd been on the receiving end and had almost forgotten how good it felt. Kyle thrust carefully, applying a little more pressure with each forward movement. Logan closed his eyes and gave himself to Kyle and the feeling that now embraced him, and suddenly Kyle was inside, gasping in pleasure, and Logan moaned.

"Oh, that's it. Keep going. Right there," he said, feeling Kyle's cock suddenly brushing his special spot, sending shockwaves of pleasure all over his body, carrying him one step closer to that final and blissfully sweet release.

Kyle leaned closer to Logan, all flushed, and Logan embraced him tightly while Kyle increased the vigor and speed of his thrusts. He moaned through his ragged breathing, "I'm gonna come!"

Logan felt a warmth inside him that pushed him over the edge. His body contracted as a wave of lust and pleasure washed over him, and he came still holding on to Kyle, his penis brushing against his stomach. They remained still for a moment, catching their breaths, reveling in the moment they'd now shared together.

"I love you," Logan said. And suddenly, he realized it was the first time he'd ever said it out loud, the first time he'd even allowed himself to think it. But he wasn't afraid. It felt right.

Kyle lifted his head, gazed at Logan and smiled. "I love you, too."

Chapter Twenty-Nine

That next Monday, Logan arrived at work with a silly grin on his face, one he just couldn't control. He was happy and his lips insisted on announcing to everyone that he was the happiest man alive. With Kyle by his side he felt he could take on the world. And not even the embarrassment he still felt from having sat next to Jessica during the previous day's dinner could deter that grin. She'd insisted on having both him and Kyle there. As Logan had felt real guilty that Jessica had waited for Kyle at his house, looking after Ryan while they'd solved their differences by having sex, he'd felt he couldn't refuse her invitation; the least he could do. That evening, he'd felt déjà vu after arriving at Kyle's house. Suddenly it was his awful dinner all over again, the three of them treading lightly around the fact that Kyle was dating Logan so little a time after Kyle and Jessica's separation. But as soon as he'd crossed the door's threshold he knew things would not be the same. There was a different energy in the air. Jessica and Kyle were talking in a relaxed manner, Ryan running around them, and she was even smiling in a way Logan felt was genuine. There was no plastic sheen in their attitude, no falsehood in their behavior. While setting the table, they seemed good friends, ones who knew each other well enough to predict what the other would need. When they all sat down to enjoy dinner, it really did feel like family. Granted, not exactly a traditional one, but family nonetheless. And Logan could even imagine that evening being the birth of a wonderful tradition.

So, yes, that Monday morning he was happier than usual, but he had good reason to be. His colleagues made sure he suffered for it, though, and kept asking him why was he smiling like an idiot all the time. At around noon, after enduring yet another fifteen-minute mocking session by a couple of his colleagues, Logan excused himself by saying he had to ask Mr. Shaffer something related to his new project. He didn't. It was a little white lie, but he didn't want to share with the guys that he was so happy simply because his boyfriend was making him happy.

"You seem awfully happy today," Mr. Shaffer said.

Logan closed the office door behind him, trying to control his smile. "I guess I'm in a good place right now but the guys can't seem to stop teasing me about it."

Mr. Shaffer chuckled. "You're hiding in here, then?"

They were interrupted when someone knocked on the door that connected the office to the front store.

"Sorry to interrupt, Mr. Shaffer," Laura, one of the sellers, said, "but there's a Mr. Chase here saying he's got an appointment with you?"

Logan felt the blood drain from his face. That Sunday had been so wonderful, and he'd felt so happy with his new family, that it had made him forget about that shady, awful man.

"Oh, yes. Send him in," Mr. Shaffer said. He waited until the door was closed again before saying to Logan, "Your new parole officer called me this weekend to set this appointment. He's...quite the character."

"He called you on a weekend?" Logan sighed, frustrated. "I don't know what he is, to be honest. He came to my house on Saturday and I could instantly tell he was nothing like Dave. He seems to despise all ex-convicts and I'm no exception. I bet he'd be glad to see me go back to jail." Logan sighed again, a dark cloud now hovering over his head. "I should go."

"No, please stay. If this Bill character is as unpleasant as he sounded on the phone, I want you to be here to know what you're dealing with."

"With all due respect, Mr. Shaffer, I don't think that's a good idea."

But before his boss could reply, someone knocked at the door again. "Come in," Mr. Shaffer said.

Laura opened the door. Behind her was Bill Chase and his unkempt mustache. He didn't seem happy to be here and barged into the office, almost running over poor Laura who wrinkled her nose at the rude man. His bad mood went into overdrive when he saw Logan was there.

"Mr. Shaffer, I presume," he said, ignoring Logan and locking eyes with Mr. Shaffer who was still sitting behind his desk. "Am I too early for our appointment?" but his politeness was clearly a sham.

"No, not at all. You're right on time," Mr. Shaffer said, standing up. "Please, take a seat."

"I was hoping we could talk alone."

Mr. Shaffer smiled. "I'm sure whatever you want to ask me Logan can hear. What can I do for you?"

Bill Chase squirmed in his chair, clearly irritated. "I'm here to evaluate Logan's performance. I understand he's been working for you for almost a year now."

"Yes, that's right."

"And has he been coming to work every day?"

"Yes. As a matter of fact, he's always the first to arrive and sets a great example for everybody. Sometimes I think he's more comfortable here than in his own home."

Bill frowned. "How about his behavior?"

"If you're asking about his manners, Logan's one of the most polite people I've ever met."

"No, that's not what I meant. Have you noticed any inventory leakage since he got here?"

Logan squinted, trying to understand what Bill had meant. Then it hit him and he was flooded by a sudden rush of adrenaline. He'd been quietly observing Bill from the corner across from him, but it was getting harder and harder not to intervene. Fortunately, Mr. Shaffer saved him from himself.

"Inventory leakage?" he said.

"Yes."

"If you're trying to imply that Logan's stolen from me, then no, he hasn't. Of course he hasn't! And it's absurd you should even consider such a possibility. He's one of my most hard-working employees, and I've recently promoted him because of that. People only have good things to say about him, and in all of the months I've got to know him he's done nothing but help people and be an honest man." Mr. Shaffer paused and Logan thought he was done answering Bill's question, but he wasn't. "I'm gonna be totally blunt here, Mr. Chase. I can sense you resent Logan for some reason I really don't understand. But no matter what you personally think, let me tell you something. I don't really care about what he did when he was young. He grew out of it. He's a man with a capital 'M' now, which is more than I can say about certain people who seem to be stuck in the past and can't act like the adult they should be."

"If you're somehow implying I'm not doing my job—"

"I'm not implying. I'm saying you should go back to school and learn how to be a decent person."

"You're not helping Logan acting like that, Mr. Shaffer. I could—"

"I don't care what you could or couldn't do. All I know is what you will do. That you'll do right by Logan or I'll make a quick phone call and you'll be out of a job faster that you can say 'Prejudiced'."

Bill looked as flushed as a tomato and seemed furious. "Are you threatening me?"

"Threatening? Look, I'm not in the mood to discuss semantics. But my patience is running thin and I'm feeling an urge to call your boss and tell her you should never have been given Dave's caseload."

Bill stood. "We'll see about that." He stormed out of the office before Logan could take in what had just happened.

"Mr. Shaffer, I'm not sure that was the right way to handle Bill. Do you think it's prudent to poke a bear like that?"

His boss turned to him. "Don't worry. I know his boss. I've known her for the past few years, actually." Mr. Shaffer paused and Logan thought he saw him blush. "She told me about Dave and how it was getting harder to find good, honest people to work as parole officers. A lot of them are just idiots who think they're going to be in a position of power. She already had some reservations about Bill and now he's just proven her completely right. Don't worry. You can trust me."

Logan nodded. He trusted Mr. Shaffer but was still worried about being at the mercy of Bill Chase.

**

"You won't believe my day," Kyle said. Logan had just arrived at his house. "Remember that guy whose work I had almost messed up?"

Logan closed the door behind him. "The guy from when you had me babysitting Ryan?"

"That's the one. He's got another job for me. I told him 'No' and gave him an excuse about having my schedule full, but he insisted and offered me triple what I usually charge. Apparently, he's in the middle of some 'Design related emergency', whatever that means. Go figure."

"That's excellent." Logan gave Kyle a quick kiss and went to the living room.

"Are you okay? You seem distant."

Logan had just perched himself on the couch. He looked up at Kyle. "I'm just worried. I'd totally forgotten about that parole officer Bill. He went to my work today to talk with Mr. Shaffer."

Kyle sat next to him. "That bad?"

"Actually, it wasn't bad, it was just…weird. Well, it was bad, but for him. He began to ask all these questions implying I was still into stealing things and then, out of nowhere, Mr. Shaffer told him off and basically accused him of being a bad professional. He practically expelled the guy from his office. I also got this weird feeling that Mr. Shaffer is dating Bill's boss, because he said he'd be talking to her about the way Bill was handling my case."

"What? Are you serious?"

"Dead serious."

"So now what?"

"I got a call from Dave on my way here. He said he'd be returning to work to be my parole officer again."

Kyle shifted on the couch. "Wait, but I thought you'd said Dave was retiring because of his health."

Logan nodded. "That's what he told me, but apparently it's just until my sentence expires."

"So he's returning just for you? Aww, how sweet of him. Why the long face, then? Isn't it better to have Dave working with you than Bill?"

"I'm just worried about Dave's health, that's all. I don't want to be the one responsible for sending him to the hospital."

Kyle smiled. "That's mighty sweet of you but I'm guessing Dave's big enough to make his own decisions. Stop worrying and focus on the good news."

Logan had been blankly staring at the wall. He blinked. "Right. Congrats on your new gig, by the way."

"Not that good news, silly," Kyle said, chuckling. "The fact that you're not going back to jail because of some idiot who dislikes former convicts."

Logan drew in a deep breath. "You know what?" he said, turning to Kyle and smiling. "You're absolutely right. I've been so wound up about the possibility of going back that being worried has become second nature. It's not easy. It's not easy starting over. Especially when you're trying to do everything different."

Kyle smiled and stroke Logan's leg. "I can't begin to imagine what it's like to be in your shoes, but I can tell you you've done an awesome job. Like Yoda said: 'Do or do not. There is no try'."

"What?"

"Yoda? From Star Wars?" Logan shrugged, completely oblivious. "Haven't you seen Star Wars? Dear lord. You have much to learn. Yoda said that you either do or you don't. Trying leads you nowhere. You have to commit yourself. And from where I stand, I'd say you've been committing a hundred percent to your new life. Everyone loves you. You really think Mrs. Cook would give you her herbs and cook for you if you were still that juvenile thief you once were? I don't think so. Plus, as Jess said, you can't fool anyone. You're pure sweetness."

Logan smiled. "You're biased. But I guess you're right."

"I am right."

Logan sighed. Just by pointing out how stressed he was, Kyle had made him aware of how much tension he carried around. Suddenly, it felt like he'd taken a heavy burden off his shoulders and the world had gained new colors. He hadn't realized just how worried he'd been since leaving jail. He'd been living in fear of making a mistake and ultimately of having his freedom revoked, and this fear had only worsened after meeting Kyle and falling for him. Going back to prison after having dabbled in freedom would be bad, sure, but after having met Kyle? Disastrous. How was he supposed to go back and forget him? Forget how he made him feel? But now, for the first time in all of these months, he realized he wasn't going anywhere. His place was here, or whatever town or city they ended up choosing to live in. And for the first time in his life, he felt like he had a future. And that future had Kyle in it.

Epilogue

Ryan was asleep on the couch, nestled between a couple of pillows and exhausted from a birthday party that had been attended by way too many kids. Logan yawned and felt tired. His bed was also calling for him but he still had to help clean the house. "Grandma" Cook, as Ryan now called Mrs. Cook, had made a delicious birthday cake that everyone had loved, especially the adults. It was delicious and tasted of custard and almond, not too sweet but plenty tasty. But now there was cake smeared on the walls and paper plates all over the place. It was a mystery to him how kids were able to make such a mess in such a short space of time. That and the amount of energy they had. Logan chuckled. He'd just remembered a joke Kyle had told him, that first day he'd had to wake up at daybreak because Ryan was awake and didn't want to sleep anymore. And, of course, if Ryan didn't want to sleep, no one else could. He'd talk and talk, and talk even more, and then he'd start to ask them why they were sleeping if there was light outside. That day, Kyle told Logan a joke he'd read somewhere. It went something like: "Someone should make a drink called Six a.m. Toddler". Logan chuckled again. Whoever had come up with it was absolutely right, they should have a drink with that name. Or someone should at least make the T-shirt. Logan would buy it.

He approached the couch and got emotional. He realized Ryan had gotten big and wasn't a little toddler anymore. These three years had flown by really fast, but he could still recall the first time his sweet boy had held on to his finger and called him "Dadda Wogan". It was so fresh in his memory. Like it had happened the previous day.

Logan picked Ryan up from the couch. The boy mumbled something about Buddy and curled his arms around Logan's neck, but didn't wake up.

"I'm gonna put him upstairs," he whispered to Kyle. He and Jess were busy clearing the table. He nodded and mouthed "Love you". Logan mouthed "Love you, too", grinning from ear to ear.

He went upstairs, Ryan's weight pressing on his shoulder. His warmth radiated through Logan and he could feel his little heart beating through his clothes, echoing on Logan's chest. Logan held him closer and kissed him on his head, and Ryan's fingers squeezed his shirt tighter. He entered Kyle's room, but instead of putting Ryan on his bed, he sat on the rocking chair he'd made three years before. He wasn't ready to let him go just yet, so he rocked the chair back and forth and hummed a song he remembered his grandma singing to him. He wanted to stay this way forever. Ryan was growing up way too fast, though, and Logan feared he'd be moving out and going to college in no time. Maybe it was time to think of the future and leave Shaffer & Hamilton Woodworks, to start his own business. He would always be eternally grateful to Mr. Shaffer for the opportunity he'd given him, but maybe it was time to move on. He wanted to give Ryan all the opportunities he deserved. He wanted him to travel and meet new people, to see the world in all its colors and traditions, to have everything he himself had been denied.

Buddy came trotting silently towards them, tongue lolling, that expression on his snout that Logan always thought was kind of a smile. He stopped right next to them and Logan petted him. Buddy had become really protective of Ryan, like an older brother. And just like an older brother, he had infinite tolerance of Ryan's nonsense.

"Hey, wanna join us? Jess is heating up some leftovers and making her famous mint tea," Kyle whispered.

Logan looked up. Kyle was standing in the doorway, smiling at them both.

"I'll be right there," he whispered back.

Kyle nodded and left. Logan stood up and went to the bed. After laying Ryan down and covering him with his comforter, he kissed him on his forehead and caressed his hair.

"I'll always be here for you, my sweet boy."

Logan had never felt love like this. He still didn't understand how anyone could not care for their children, but he knew he would never not care. He kissed Ryan again. "I'll always be here for you. No matter what."

He signaled Buddy to go with him, turned off the lights and closed the door behind them. His little boy was growing up fast. He put that thought away for the moment. One step at a time. Now, he was starving and the smell of pot roast was making his mouth water.

THE END

23540414R00117

Printed in Great Britain
by Amazon